*Yours
Forever*

Yours Forever

ROBIN JONES GUNN

BETHANY HOUSE PUBLISHERS
MINNEAPOLIS, MINNESOTA 55438

Yours Forever
Revised edition 1998
Copyright © 1990, 1998
Robin Jones Gunn

Edited by Janet Kobobel
Cover illustration and design by the Lookout Design Group

Published by Bethany House Publishers
11400 Hampshire Avenue South
Bloomington, Minnesota 55438

Bethany House Publishers is a division of
Baker Publishing Group, Grand Rapids, Michigan.

Printed in the United States of America

ISBN 1-56179-599-2

04 05 06 07 08 09 10 / 19 18 17 16 15 14 13 12 11 10 9

To my favorite man of God, my husband,

Ross Gunn III

We are His forever.

Contents

CHAPTER ONE

The Gift

"See, Katie! I told you he wouldn't be here," 15-year-old Christy Miller whispered, standing stiffly in the corner of the gym.

"Trust me, Christy. Rick told me he was coming to church tonight to play basketball. He'll be here." Katie's copper-colored hair swished as she quickly glanced over her shoulder, checking the entrance.

"Well, even if he does come, I'm not going to give him this Christmas present. It was a bad idea." Christy slipped the small gift into the purse slung over her shoulder.

"No it wasn't!"

"Yes it was, Katie. I hardly know Rick, so why am I chasing after him to give him a present?" Christy felt her face getting hot. She felt hot all over. Quickly running a finger over each eyelid, she asked, "Is my eye makeup all smeared?"

Katie looked into Christy's distinctive blue-green eyes. "No, not at all. I can't even tell you have any on."

"Maybe I should go in the bathroom and put on some more."

"Christy, stop with the Barbie Beauty Shop, will you? You're a natural beauty—and Rick knows it." Katie put her hand on her hip. "As long as you've known Rick Doyle, you've been running

1

away from him. Now that he's finally showing some interest in you, why don't you stand still long enough for him to catch you?"

Christy looked around, avoiding the question. The truth was, Rick could melt her with a single look. She was fine around him as long as they were teasing each other. But standing here, waiting for him like this, pushed her out of her comfort zone.

The church gym began to echo with the thump, thump of basketballs and loud hoots and calls of the athletes warming up for the usual Friday rec night. The only other girls Christy noticed were sitting in a clump on the bleachers.

"Katie, I wish we hadn't come." Christy fingered her shoulder-length, nutmeg brown hair. "I'm not into sports, like you. I feel totally out of place here."

Katie's face suddenly lit up. "Don't turn around," she muttered under her breath, "but there he is!"

Christy's heart felt as though it was thump-thumping as loudly as the basketballs that pounded the gym floor. "Did he see us? Is he coming over here?"

Katie looked pleased. "The answer is yes and yes, and you're on your own now. I'll see you later."

"Katie!" Christy called out as her friend jogged across the court, scooped up a basketball, and filed into line with a bunch of free-throwers.

"Hi," came a deep voice from behind Christy.

She turned slowly, letting her gaze melt into Rick's chocolate brown eyes. His dark hair looked especially good tonight, all wavy on the sides.

"Hi," she answered, feeling petite at five-foot-seven in the shadow of his six-foot-four-inch frame.

"Katie said you were coming tonight."

"And you came just to see me, right?" Christy switched from

her nervousness to the lighthearted, flirty way she had been talking lately with Rick.

He played right along. "I've been counting the seconds."

"Oh yeah? How many did you count?"

"Billions."

"I didn't know you could count that high," Christy teased.

Rick playfully grabbed her by the elbow. "Is that any way to talk to the only guy here who brought you a Christmas present?"

"You did?" Christy felt her cheeks flush with surprise. Maybe what everyone had been telling her was true. Maybe Rick really did like her.

"Maybe I brought you a present and maybe I didn't." Rick grinned. "All depends. Have you been a good girl this year?"

"Oh, yes, Santa. I've been very good."

"In that case, you'd better come out to my sleigh and get your present. Especially since my elves tell me you're leaving town tomorrow."

"My whole family is going to my aunt and uncle's in Newport Beach. But we'll be gone only a week."

"A week!" Rick clutched his chest as if he were having a heart attack. "Do you know how many billions of seconds are in a week?"

Christy laughed. "No, how many?"

"I don't know. That's why I asked you. I can't count that high, remember?"

Christy playfully swatted Rick on the shoulder, then followed him out of the gym and into the parking lot. It was a mild Southern California evening. Rick had on shorts and a gray sweatshirt. Christy felt overdressed in her black pants and white silk shirt, buttoned up to the collar. Christy had seen a girl at school wearing an outfit like hers that week, and she thought it looked good. That's why she tried to copy the outfit tonight. She thought it might help her capture Rick's attention. Apparently, she didn't need a particular outfit to do that.

They batted jokes back and forth on their way to Rick's cherry red Mustang. Ever since he had given her a ride home from church over two months ago, she had watched for his car everywhere—at school, at church. It was usually full of guys and girls, and Rick was so busy with his fan club that he never noticed Christy watching from afar.

Then two weeks ago he talked to her at church, and for some reason they started this game of who could tease the other one the most. They had talked to each other every day since then, and people had started to ask Christy if they were going out.

Now, standing at the far end of the parking lot in front of Rick's car, it seemed unusually quiet after all the hubbub in the gym. Rick unlocked the front door, bent over, and grabbed a box wrapped with a huge red ribbon.

"For you," he said.

"You shouldn't have, Rick."

"I know. I know."

"Should I open it now?" She felt excited and full of anticipation—and relieved she had a present for him, too.

"Sure. Go ahead. Live dangerously," Rick said, folding his arms across his chest. "To be honest, I didn't know what to get you. My sister suggested a book. She said most girls like to read."

Christy opened the box, and sure enough, it was a book. She held it up to read the title in the faint light: *One Hundred-Twelve Uses for a Dead Hamster*. Her emotions did a nosedive.

What kind of present is this? Does Rick actually think I'd like a joke book for a Christmas present?

Rick grinned. "I got one of the few copies left. It's bound to be a best-seller this Christmas."

"Rick, you're a sick person!" Christy felt like throwing his morbid book at him.

"Check out number 15," Rick said, turning the pages for her. "This is my favorite. See, you bend a coat hanger between two of them, and you've got ear muffs."

Christy didn't look at the illustration. She glared up at Rick.

Rick caught her look and held it a moment; then he thumped his forehead with the palm of his hand and said, "Oh, man! How could I have been so stupid? You already have this book, right?"

Christy burst out laughing. "You are so strange, Rick Doyle! You have to be the strangest person on the face of this earth."

"That's why I need someone like you. Someone who's pretty and charming and whose manners might rub off on me."

Christy stopped laughing. She stood perfectly still, looking up at him, her blue-green eyes searching his in the dim light. How did he do that? Tease her mercilessly and then compliment her in the same breath.

"You really are," Rick said. "Charming, I mean." He moved a little closer to Christy and in a hushed voice said, "Actually, what I really wanted to give you I couldn't put in a box."

"Oh yeah?" Christy felt her stomach tighten. She wasn't used to being serious with Rick. "What was that?"

"This." Rick grasped her by the shoulders, bent down, and kissed her. Then he stood up straight and looked around, as if to make sure no one had seen them.

Christy swallowed and tried not to look as though the most shocking thing in the world had just happened to her. *Why did he do that? Now what? What should I say? What should I do?*

Rick stood firm, waiting for Christy's response.

"I, um, I have a present for you, too," she said.

"Oh yeah?" He smiled one of his half-face grins in which only the left side of his mouth curved upward.

"Here." Christy pulled the wrapped compact disc from her purse and handed it to him. "I hope you don't already have this one."

The grin disappeared.

Is he disappointed that I ignored his kiss? Should I have waited longer before giving him the gift? Christy felt awkward and not at all charming.

Rick pulled the wrapping off and said with mild enthusiasm, "Oh, thanks. I don't have this one."

The weird, confusing feelings that had overwhelmed her when Rick kissed her began to evaporate. She imagined they would walk back to the gym now, both acting as though nothing out of the ordinary had happened. They would be just friends again and would go back to their flirty little games. It would be fun again instead of puzzling.

"Thanks a lot, Christy. That was really nice of you," Rick said, tossing the CD onto his front seat and locking the car door. He stuck the keys in his pocket and said in a low voice, "I was kind of hoping your present didn't come in a box either."

Her heart began to pound. *He wants me to kiss him! But do I want to kiss him? Did I even want him to kiss me the first time? Or is this part of our game, and now it's my turn to make a move if I want to keep the game going?* Before Christy could tie all her thoughts together, Rick leaned over and kissed her. This time it was longer than the first kiss.

Christy pulled away quickly. He was coming at her too fast. This was too confusing. What was he thinking? She lowered her head, and Rick let go. They stood there, silent, while Christy's heart and mind raced with mixed messages.

"Well," Rick said, clearing his throat, "I guess we'd better get back in." He nodded his head toward the gym. His expression showed that he was hurt. Or angry. Or both. Christy didn't know what to say. They walked quickly, with a tight strain between them.

The rest of the evening seemed to go on around Christy in slow motion as she kept replaying the scene in the parking lot. What had gone wrong? She liked Rick. All the girls liked him. She loved being around him and having people see them together. She loved teasing him and the way he joked with her. He had a personality like no other guy she had ever known. And he was so good-looking. He made her feel pretty when he looked at her.

And, yes, she had dreamed about what it would be like to kiss him. But in her dreams, it was nothing like the way it turned out tonight. In her dreams, the kiss was sweet and innocent and romantic—like it had been last summer when Todd kissed her the day she left Newport Beach. She and Todd had stood in the middle of the street with the whole world watching, and she had felt all warm and glowy inside.

With Rick, she felt surprised and confused and as if they were hiding from the whole world in the dark parking lot. She wasn't ready for what had just happened.

Christy didn't take her eyes off Rick all night as he played basketball. But he never once looked her way. Was he confused, too? Or was he mad at her? Had she ruined everything by not responding in a way that would let him know she liked him?

Determined to say something before she left, Christy positioned herself only a few feet from the exit and waited. Rick brushed past her, arguing with the guy next to him over who was supposed to be covering whom on the last play. Rick didn't even look at her.

The worst part was Katie's prodding on the way home. "So, he gave you a stupid book and then what?"

"I gave him the CD." Christy wasn't about to say any more, especially with Katie's mom listening as she drove the car.

"Well, did he like it?"

"He said he did."

"Then what was the problem with you two tonight? He didn't even say good-bye or anything when he left. And you were only standing a few feet away from him."

"It's no big deal. We're just friends," Christy said defensively.

"So . . ." Katie paused before switching subjects. "When do you leave for your aunt and uncle's?"

"Tomorrow. We'll be back on New Year's or the day after."

"Did Todd ever call? Are you going to see him next week?"

"I don't know, Katie. He hasn't called yet." The words stung as Christy said them, and Katie backed off again.

The two girls had gotten into an argument just last week over Todd. Katie told Christy to forget him, since he hadn't called or written in months, and she told Christy to go after Rick, since he was suddenly interested in her.

Christy argued that her relationship with Todd was so solid that even if she didn't see him for months, they could still pick up where they had left off last summer. Nothing would have changed between them.

Now reality was about to hit. Tomorrow she had to get in the car with her mom, dad, and eight-year-old brother, David, and drive the hour and a half from Escondido to Uncle Bob and Aunt Marti's house in Newport Beach. Todd would be there, living at his dad's house.

Then what would happen? Would Todd remember that he called her in October and promised they would have breakfast together on the beach? Would everything still be the same between them? And what would happen with Rick while she was gone?

When she got home, Christy retreated to her bedroom. There she lifted an old Folgers coffee can from her dresser and poured

out a mound of dried carnations onto her yellow patchwork comforter. The faint scent of coffee came tumbling out with what was
left of the bouquet of white carnations Todd had given her the
day he kissed her.

Twirling one of the withered petals between her thumb and
forefinger, Christy whispered, "Lord, what's going to happen with
Todd? What should I do about Rick? Everything seemed fine
until tonight. Does stuff like this even matter to You? Of course
it does. What am I saying? It's just that You don't speak to me
and tell me what I'm supposed to do. That would make it a whole
lot easier, You know."

Christy paused and pressed the flower against her cheek. "I
want a second chance with Rick. I want to start over and not let
everything get all weird. And I want everything with Todd to be
just like it was last summer. That's all I want for Christmas, Lord.
Oh, and one more thing. I want to make You happy. I mean, I
don't want to mess up and make You or anybody else disappointed with me."

Christy got ready for bed, wondering if she should have
prayed the way she just did, giving God a wish list as if He were
Santa Claus. *At least I was honest,* she thought. *I don't want to hide
anything from God. Doesn't He already know everything?*

Christy slipped between the cool sheets and curled up with
the comforter tucked under her chin, clutching in her right hand
a withered carnation.

CHAPTER TWO

A Promise Kept

"You about ready, Christy?" Christy's dad rapped on her bedroom door.

"I'll be right there." Christy grabbed her purse and a bag with cosmetics and hurried out to the car.

Christy's mom, a short, round woman, stood by the front door, brushing back a strand of graying hair. "Norman," she called to Christy's dad, "you'd better take your Bible. I don't know if Bob and Marti have one in their house."

"Maybe that's what we should have gotten them instead of that box of international cheeses," Dad called back in his deep voice.

Christy could tell he was teasing. Her mom had tried so hard to come up with a nice gift for Bob and Marti, the couple who had everything. When Mom came home from the mall with a big gift-wrapped box of international cheeses, for some reason, Dad thought it was hilarious and had teased her for days.

"Christy," Mom said, ignoring Dad's joke, "will you put the rest of these things in the car and tell your brother to get ready to go?"

Christy found David climbing a tree in the backyard and coaxed him down. A big kid with reddish-brown hair, he resembled their father. David had begun wearing glasses a few weeks earlier and had developed an annoying habit of scrunching up his nose to keep them from sliding off.

Christy thought it looked disgusting and kept saying, "David, don't do that!"

He would only scrunch and squint more and say, "Don't do what?" He did it about 20 times in the car during the drive up the coast to Bob and Marti's.

Finally, Christy said, "You look like a hamster, David."

"I do not!" he spouted. "Mom, Christy called me a hamster!"

"Please don't start, you two. We'll be there soon. Just look at the ocean. Isn't it beautiful? Such a unique color today—almost like gray glass," Mom said.

"I miss the snow." David stuck out his lower lip in a pout. "Doesn't seem like Christmas without the snow."

"That's because you never spent Christmas day shoveling the driveway for four hours," his dad said. "I don't miss it a bit."

Mom smiled. She reached over and squeezed her husband's shoulder. Christy felt warm inside. She hadn't seen her parents this content in years. Things had been awfully hard for them back on the farm in Wisconsin. Since they had moved to Escondido in September, their family had gotten much closer. Christy noticed the biggest changes in her parents after they started going to church and joined a home Bible study group. They were settled and happy.

"Can I go out on the beach as soon as we get there?" David asked.

"We'll see," Mom said.

Uncle Bob greeted them at the door of his beautiful house in Newport Beach. "Welcome, welcome! Merry Christmas! Come on in!" He had on a red vest and a matching bow tie with white lights that blinked off and on.

"Hey, cool!" David said, reaching up to touch the bow tie. "How does it do that?"

Bob patted his right pants pocket, where he had a small box with batteries. Then he lifted his vest to reveal the wire leading up to the tie.

"We special-effects guys never give away our secrets," he said with a wink to David. "But we just might have another one of these gizmos lying around. You never know."

Marti rushed up behind Bob. "Why didn't you tell me they were here, darling? Come in, come in." She wore a festive sweater that was black with a Christmas tree woven into the front and trimmed in silver with a star on top. Her earrings were little presents that matched the ones under the tree on her sweater.

Christy glanced at her family, all dressed in jeans and crumpled sweatshirts. Familiar feelings of inferiority and embarrassment spread over her. But her mom didn't seem to be ruffled, so Christy decided to not let it bother her either.

They stepped into the living room, and all admired the elegant decorations. Everything was white, including a new leather couch and love seat. White and silver garlands hung across the huge window and fireplace mantle. And in front of the window stood a magnificent white-flocked tree, loaded with tiny silver balls and lamb ornaments. Dozens of gifts poured out from its base.

"Christy, remember when we picked out all these lamb ornaments in San Francisco last summer? Didn't it turn out adorable?"

"It's really pretty, Aunt Marti," Christy said sweetly. Inwardly, she missed the smell of evergreen and the homemade strings of popcorn and cranberries that laced their small tree at home.

"We brought our nativity scene," Christy said. "Could we put it up on the coffee table?"

"I suppose so," Marti said slowly. "As long as it doesn't scratch the glass, dear."

"I'll be careful."

While Dad carried in the luggage, and Mom busied herself in the kitchen, Christy set up the nativity scene. She kept glancing out the huge windows at the view of the beach. Her mind flooded with thoughts of Todd. Where was he now? When would he call? Would he stop by? Would they have breakfast on the beach as he promised? Escondido and Rick and Katie all seemed far, far away. Todd and all her summer beach friends were all that mattered right now.

The family gathered around the kitchen table for soup and salad.

"I planned a light dinner," Marti explained as they sipped their French onion soup. "We have so much snack food around here, I knew we'd be nibbling all night. So many of our friends gave us food this year. And some store must have had a sale on cheese because we've been given three boxes of international cheeses!"

Dad tried to suppress a choking laugh, but he couldn't do it. He sprayed his spoonful of soup into his napkin and then tilted his head back and roared a contagious laugh. David laughed wildly and fell off his chair for added attention. Christy giggled uncontrollably. Poor Mom looked as though she were about to cry. Then slowly, she began to chuckle along with the rest of them.

"Was it something I said?" Marti looked bewildered, not sure if they were laughing at her or at something she had accidentally said. She looked to Bob for support.

Gentle, wise Bob calmly sipped his soup and said, "Perhaps we'll understand when we open their gift tonight." He winked at

Christy's mom. "I like the Brie, myself."

Marti still looked confused, but as soon as everyone stopped laughing, she carried on as if she were still completely in control of the situation. "I thought we'd open all the gifts tonight. That way we can sleep in tomorrow morning, and we'll have a lovely Christmas dinner at 1:00. What time do you need to get back to Escondido?"

"We both have to work the next day, so we should try to leave by 5:00 or 6:00," Mom said.

"Which reminds me," Dad said, leaning across the table and wagging his soup spoon at Christy and David. "You two keep in mind that you're guests of your aunt and uncle this next week. They didn't have to invite you, you know. You need to make sure you do your best to fit into their plans, all right?"

They both nodded.

"Good," Dad said, and he stuck his spoon back into his soup.

Christy's mind left the family conversation and constructed elaborate dreams of when she would see Todd and what it would be like.

That evening, the family gathered by the fire in the living room. Before they dove into the mound of presents, Christy's dad offered to read the Christmas story from the Gospel of Luke. He had done this every year since Christy could remember, and she nearly had the passage memorized. This year it was different. Not just because they were at Bob and Marti's, but because this year she really knew Jesus. To her, He wasn't just a little baby in a manger anymore. Last summer she had surrendered her life to Him and promised Him her whole heart. Jesus was real to Christy. His Spirit lived inside her.

"That was lovely," Marti said when Dad finished reading. "It's good for us to remember the true meaning of Christmas." Instantly, she sat upright and pointed to a small package in the front. "David, you open that one first, all right, dear? We looked all over town for this one," she confided to Christy's mom. "I couldn't believe how the price had gone up since three years ago when I got Bob's, but I knew David would want one."

David tore open the box and pulled out his own flashing bow tie. "All right!" he cheered. "How do you hook it up, Uncle Bob?"

And that's how it began. Over two hours of wrapping paper flying and expensive gifts emerging, one right after the other. Next to Christy, on the couch, sat a pile of wonderful gifts— clothes, perfume, makeup, a compact disc player, and a Walkman. Although she thought it was all very nice, something felt hollow. She had been through all this money-and-clothes thing with her aunt and uncle in the past, and she never felt really good about it. Right now she wished her dad would read the part about the angels and shepherds again.

She felt kind of bad, too, because nobody seemed overly excited about the T-shirts she gave them. She and another friend from Escondido, Janelle, had gone to a craft store and bought the paint, stencils, and big T-shirts. It cost every penny she had just for the supplies. For three days, she and Janelle had worked on designing and painting the shirts. They had a great time working on them, and Christy had felt pleased at how they had turned out.

But now, watching Marti hold up the T-shirt with the large yellow sunflower carefully painted on the front, Christy knew it was a waste. Her aunt would never wear it. David liked his shirt, though, with the neon-colored surfer splashed across the front.

Then Bob lifted an envelope off one of the flocked branches of the tree and handed it to Christy. "Merry Christmas to our favorite niece," he said.

It was a bankbook, a savings account in her name, and printed in the ledger was the amount: "$10,000.00." Christy swallowed hard and showed the bankbook to her parents.

"Bob," Dad said in gruff voice, "this is going too far. We can't accept this." He looked hurt and angry at the same time.

"Let me explain," Bob said smoothly. "One of my real estate investments out in Rancho California paid off exceptionally well this year. I thought it would be profitable for me to reinvest the money into a very promising, worthwhile cause, namely, Christy's future. I set this up as a college fund. She can't touch the money until she's 18. I don't see how any kid can get into a decent college these days without some little nest egg stored away."

Mom looked as though she might cry.

Dad still looked angry.

"Believe me," Bob said, "you're doing me a favor. It's either a scholarship account or else I have to pay exorbitant taxes on it."

Mom smiled at her husband.

He said in a hoarse voice, "Thanks, Bob."

Christy rose and kissed Uncle Bob on the cheek. "Thank you," she said with a smile.

"What a rip!" David said. "All that money, and she can't even touch it until she's 18!"

"David!" Mom scolded.

Bob laughed and pulled another envelope from the tree. "This 'rip' is for you, David. You can't touch yours until you're 18 either! I figure during the next decade, this will pull in some favorable interest for you."

"Wow! Five thousand bucks!" David said, looking at the total. "Couldn't I just take a little bit of it out to buy a new bike?"

"No!" his parents said in unison.

"Bob," Marti said brightly, "why don't you give David his last gift?"

Bob pulled a small wrapped box off a top branch and handed it to David. He tore it open and pulled out a piece of paper, then read the note aloud. "Go to the closet in the hallway and see what Santa left for you."

They all followed David to the hall closet. He opened it up, and on the floor was a big bow with a long ribbon attached. The ribbon ran up and over the doorway and across the kitchen floor.

"This is cool!" David shouted. They all followed him through the kitchen, in and out of the dining room, back through the kitchen, through the laundry room, and into the garage. There, in the center of the garage, stood a new bike with a big white bow on it. David whooped and hollered, and there was so much commotion that when Bob turned to Christy and said, "Would you get the phone for me? It's probably your grandmother," Christy strained to hear if it was really ringing. She grabbed it in the kitchen and answered full of cheer: "Merry Christmas!"

"Hey, how's it going?"

"Todd?"

"Yeah, hi. How's it going?"

"Hi! Are you at your dad's house?"

"Yeah."

"Are you having a merry Christmas?" *That sounded so dumb!*

"Pretty good. Hey, you want to have breakfast on the beach tomorrow morning?"

"On Christmas morning?"

"Sure. Unless you have family plans in the morning. I thought I'd give it a shot."

"Yeah, I mean, no. Everyone was going to sleep in. Let me ask my parents real quick, okay? Hold on."

Christy scurried to the garage, breathless. How was she going to ask this? Would her parents understand how much this meant to her?

"Mom?" Christy broke into the group of adults as they watched David ride around in circles in the cleared garage. "Mom, one of my friends from the summer is on the phone, and they want to know if I could have breakfast with them tomorrow morning."

"On Christmas morning?"

"Well, I thought you guys were going to sleep in tomorrow."

Marti nudged her way into the conversation. "That's right. That's what we planned. I don't see why you couldn't go."

"Where are you going to eat breakfast?" Mom asked.

"On the beach. We were going to cook it out on the beach."

"I don't know, Christy." Mom hesitated.

Bob stuck his head over and said in a calm voice, "It's perfectly safe. You can see the fire pits from our living room window."

"I suppose it's all right; I'll have to ask your father. Norm?" Mom turned to get her husband's attention. "Christy wants to go out on the beach in the morning with some of her friends—for breakfast. Is that all right with you?"

"Why in the world do you want to do that?" Dad turned to look at Christy.

She glanced at her mom and Bob and Marti. They all were looking at her dad with favorable expressions on their faces. Bob was nodding his okay.

"Oh, I don't care," Dad said. "Whatever your mother says."

Christy dashed back to the phone. "Todd? Are you still there?"

"Yes."

"It's okay. I can do it. What time, and what do you want me to bring?"

"Is 7:00 too early?"

"No. That's fine. What should I bring?"

"I went to the store already and got bacon and eggs and

orange juice, and we've got plenty of firewood here. I guess all you need to bring is yourself."

Christy smiled. "Okay. I'm really looking forward to seeing you, Todd."

"It'll be good to see you, too. I'd better let you get back to your family. I didn't mean to interrupt anything."

"You didn't. That's okay. I'll see you tomorrow morning."

"Later," Todd said and hung up.

Christy held the receiver to her ear, listening to the dial tone. She whispered into the mouthpiece, "Good-bye, Todd. I'll see you tomorrow."

CHAPTER THREE

December Dawn

"What do you mean I have to take David with me?" Christy squawked.

"Your father and I thought it would be good for David to meet some of your friends. He doesn't know anyone here, and since you're both spending the week with Bob and Marti, we thought he should have a chance to make some friends."

"But, Mom," Christy said cautiously, "there won't be anybody there his age. I don't think he would have a good time. Really!"

"Then it's up to you to see to it that he does have a good time. Our decision is final. Either you both go to this crazy breakfast on the beach, or neither of you goes! What's your choice, Christina?"

"I guess David will go with me," Christy said slowly.

"Fine," her mom said, squeezing her arm and heading for the bedroom door. "Sweet dreams. And have fun in the morning."

Mom closed the door, leaving Christy alone in the bedroom that had been hers during her summer stay with Bob and Marti. She slipped under the flannel sheets and gave her pillow a few well-aimed karate chops.

"This is so unfair!" she muttered. "David is going to ruin

everything! This was supposed to be just for Todd and me. I've waited weeks and weeks for this breakfast, and now David is going to ruin everything!"

Deep down, she knew it was her fault. She had stretched the truth with her parents by making it sound as though the breakfast was with a bunch of friends, not with just Todd. If they knew it was only Todd, they wouldn't let her go. Or would they? Rather than coming right out and asking, she had covered up the real plan, and now she was facing the consequences.

Nevertheless, she was going to see Todd in only a few hours. She couldn't let anything ruin that. Not even David. Why did Todd wait until the last minute to call her? Why was he always so easygoing and noncommittal?

Todd, you are so unpredictable! You frustrate me to pieces. Why do I feel so many deep, strong emotions toward you? What is it going to be like to see you tomorrow? Are you going to hug me? Are we going to be able to have good, long talks like we did last summer? Do you even care about me at all?

"Of course he does," Christy answered aloud. "He called, didn't he? He kept his promise about the breakfast. He even bought the food already. See, he likes you. He's been looking forward to seeing you. Don't be so insecure!"

She coaxed herself to sleep, concentrating on Todd—what he would look like after almost five months, how she would greet him, what she would wear, what they would talk about.

She smiled. As a child she had dozed off to sleep on Christmas Eve with dreams of a new toy. Tonight she was dreaming bigger dreams—more complicated, but much more exciting. She would awaken, not to Santa Claus and his gifts, but to Todd and breakfast on the beach.

At 5:30, the alarm's shrill buzz rousted her from her sweet dreams. She wanted to sleep 10 more minutes, but she didn't dare. It took more than an hour to shower and get ready. Then Christy put on some of the new eye shadow Marti had given her for Christmas. She tried the lavenders and browns but decided they made her look dull and groggy. Quickly washing the colors off, she went for three shades of very light green and a dark eyeliner. It was more than she usually wore, but she wanted to look her best. Older. *Will Todd notice?* she wondered.

Choosing what to wear was easy. Aunt Marti had given her a sweater she fell in love with the minute she pulled it out of the box. It was ivory and soft and very Christmas-y feeling. Christy slipped on her favorite pair of jeans and the new sweater. She felt snuggly and romantic—ready to see Todd.

"David, wake up!" Christy said, standing beside the hide-a-bed in the den, where her brother lay, sound asleep.

"Go away."

"Fine." Christy began to tiptoe away, her mind spinning with a plan. If she tried to wake David, but he wouldn't get up, then it wouldn't be her fault that he didn't go out on the beach with her, would it?

Suddenly, David popped his head up. "Wait a minute! We're supposed to go to the beach, huh?"

Rats! "Yes, David. Are you coming or not?"

"What's that smell?"

"What smell?"

"It smells like stinky flowers."

Christy sniffed and realized he had caught a whiff of her new Amazon Gardenia perfume. She had sprayed it in her hair and on her clothes so it would last. Maybe she had overdone it a bit.

"Just get going, David. I'm leaving in five minutes. You'd better be ready."

He sprang from the bed and hollered, "I will, I will. Close the door."

Christy popped her head into the kitchen. Uncle Bob was already up and was putting together a picnic basket.

"What are you doing?" Christy asked, surprised to see him up.

"Good morning, Bright Eyes. Don't you look terrific." He sniffed the air. "You smell pretty . . . ah . . . pretty"—he gave an impromptu cough—"pretty. That's it. You smell pretty."

Christy laughed. "I think most of it will blow away in the morning air, once I get outside."

"Let's hope so—I mean, I imagine so." Bob winked. "I tossed a few goodies into this basket for you and your friends. Hope it's enough. I didn't know how many of your friends were going this morning."

Christy felt horribly guilty. "Uncle Bob? Can I tell you something?"

Bob stopped filling the basket to give Christy his full attention. "Of course you can."

"Well, a couple of months ago Todd called me. He was still in Florida then. He said he was moving back here to live with his dad. See, his mom was getting remarried and moving to New York. Anyway, he asked me if I wanted to have breakfast on the beach with him. Then he never called again, until last night."

Uncle Bob smiled. "And you were afraid your parents wouldn't let you go alone, so you made it sound as if the whole group would be there. Am I right?"

Christy nodded.

"Somehow I thought that might be the situation." Bob reached over and squeezed Christy's hand. "Listen, I talked with your folks about it last night after they told you David was going with you. I put in a good word for Todd. They figured it would be okay, since David would be with you. But, Christy, you need to know that it hurt your parents. You're making it difficult for them to trust you. I expect more from you. Your parents deserve more than you're giving them."

By now Christy had shed big tears that dripped down her cheeks, leaving streaks from the eyeliner. She felt awful. In barely a whisper she asked, "What should I do?"

Bob straightened up, his expression tender. "Go for it, Christy. Go have a wonderful breakfast. When you get a chance this afternoon, tell your parents the whole story. They'll understand. They were teenagers once."

David pushed open the kitchen door and headed for a box of candy on the counter. "When are we going?" he asked, stuffing two chocolates into his mouth.

Christy grabbed a paper towel and dried her eyes. "I'm almost ready."

"One more spot on the side of your cheek," Bob said as Christy dabbed the last streak of runaway eye makeup.

"There, you got it. You look great."

Christy gave him an "Are-you-totally-sure?" look.

He winked. "I like you better as a natural beauty anyway. The blue in your eyes needs no competition."

She felt a little better.

"Here's a blanket for you to sit on, and this Thermos is full of steaming cocoa. My own recipe," Bob said. "The mugs are in the basket with the croissants and fruit."

Christy scooped up the gear in her arms.

"Come on, David," she called, "let's go!"

David stuffed two more pieces of candy into his mouth and mumbled, "Okay, okay!" Then he grabbed four more chocolates and waved his full fist at Uncle Bob.

"Thank you, Uncle Bob," Christy said, tossing the blanket at David. "Here. Carry this."

"Aw, do I have to?" David complained, his paws full of candy.

"Would you rather carry this basket and Thermos?"

"No," he mumbled, stuffing the blanket under his arm and stepping into the early morning mist with his sister.

The Christmas morning sky matched the creamy blue-gray of the foaming ocean. The air, the sand, even the quick breaths Christy took, felt damp and chilly.

"Lord," she whispered, "I'm sorry I messed things up. I don't want to hide stuff from my parents, and I especially don't want to hide stuff from You. I'm sorry."

She took a deep breath, filling her lungs with moist morning air and her heart with anticipation. Then she stopped.

There he was!

Tall, broad-shouldered, blond, wearing shorts and a navy blue hooded sweatshirt, Todd bent over the fire pit, poking the logs.

Christy started meshing her feet faster through the sand, David following right behind her. There Todd stood, only a few yards away, yet she couldn't get a single word out of her heart, through her mouth, and into the space that hung between them.

Suddenly, David called out, "Hey, dude!"

Todd spun around.

"David! Why did you say that?" Christy scolded.

"That's what surfers say. I saw it on TV."

Christy looked up. Only a few feet away stood a confident, grinning Todd. Christy halted. Everything she had ever felt for him rolled itself into a big wad and landed in the pit of her stomach. She couldn't say a word.

Todd only grinned. Then he looked at David. "Hey, how's it going, dude?"

"See, Christy?" David said proudly. "I told you all surfers say 'dude.'"

Todd laughed. "So, what's your name, dude?"

"David."

"You ever gone out on a skim board, dude?" Todd said playfully.

"You mean in the water?"

"C'mere, dude. I'll teach ya."

Todd flashed a wide smile at Christy. His screaming silver-blue eyes pierced hers. Then he turned, slid the oval fiberglass board under his arm, and threw his other arm around David's shoulders. The two of them trotted down to the water.

Christy stood perfectly still. *Wait a minute! What's happening here? Todd! What are you doing, taking off with my pesky little brother and leaving me here like this?* Christy still held the basket and blanket in her arms. *I should have dropped these the moment I saw you! I should have dropped this junk and run into your arms and hugged you the way I planned it in my dream last night.*

Now here she stood, alone, hugging her stupid blanket. *Come on, Christy. Get a grip. Act busy, like you're having fun. They'll be back up in a minute.*

She set to work, spreading out the blanket and surveying the food situation. Her mind scrambled to construct a Plan B in which she would be the center of attention, not David. Within a few minutes, she had found everything she needed, stretched out the bacon strips in the frying pan, and placed it on the grill.

She kept glancing down the shore to where Todd was demonstrating the skim-board technique. He would wait until a wave receded, then he would toss the board on the wet sand, run, jump on it, and skid a few feet down the shoreline before the next wave came. As it receded, he would go through the same steps all over again.

Todd looked taller and more athletic than she had remembered. His hair was a darker shade of blond than in the summer, but he still wore it short. Watching him at this distance made it seem as though she were watching a home video, not actually preparing their dream breakfast on the beach.

The popping bacon called her attention back to the fire. It smelled great. Christy carefully turned each strip, making sure none of it got too well done. It looked as though Todd had remembered everything: plates, silverware, even paper towels to drain the bacon. The eggs were hard to crack. Maybe because her fingers were slick from the bacon grease. But once in the frying pan, scrambled around, the eggs cooked extremely fast. Christy felt like a little pioneer woman and couldn't wait for Todd to see.

"Hey, dudes!" Christy yelled down the beach. They didn't respond. She walked closer to them and hollered again. They still didn't hear her. She glanced up and down the beach. Not another soul was out this morning. "Come on, you guys!"

They heard her and waved, but kept on skim-boarding.

"Come on!" she yelled, waving for them to come. Then she whistled loudly and stood there, emphasizing the point with her hands on her hips.

They finally obliged, and Todd, red-cheeked and out of breath, jogged up to her, the wet board under his arm. He slipped his free arm around her shoulder and gave her a quick hug. Everything inside her shivered. Without saying anything, Christy slipped her arm around his waist, and they headed toward the fire pit, lost in a dream.

Suddenly, Todd let go and took off running and shouting, waving his arm over his head,

"What's wrong?" Christy called out after him. David came running up beside her, and together she and David ran to the fire pit. "What happened?"

"Seagulls," Todd said, holding up a paper plate with only one strip of bacon left. "Guess they thought it was their Christmas present."

"Oh, no!" Christy cried. "Look at the eggs! They ruined everything!"

Overhead, the gulls circled, their shrill appeals for more, more, more, piercing the air.

"Hey, it's cool," Todd said. "We've still got some orange juice."

"But, Todd," Christy said, trying hard not to cry, "everything was perfect!"

"I already ate," David said, the telltale chocolate marks lining his lower lip. "Can I go use your skim board some more?"

"Sure, dude," Todd said, chomping into the slice of bacon. He turned to Christy. "Not bad. No wonder the birds liked it."

He looked so content—so unruffled by the catastrophe. It frustrated Christy, yet set her at ease at the same time.

"I just remembered!" she said. "My uncle packed some stuff." She lifted the lid to the basket. "There's plenty in here, look! Do you like croissants?"

"Sure. What's this?" Todd held up a foil wedge of Dutch Gouda. Christy laughed and told Todd the story of the abundance of international cheese at Bob and Marti's.

He smiled, and she could see his dimples. Stretching out on the blanket, he broke open a croissant and smeared it with strawberry jam. He propped his wet feet up by the fire and said, "Good morning, Lord Jesus! Are You having a good birthday?"

Christy didn't know if she should close her eyes and bow her head or look up into the sky, the way Todd was. She had never heard anyone pray like this before, but then Todd wasn't like anybody else. And the way he talked to God wasn't like anybody else either.

Todd finished with, "Amen," and then chomped into the flaky croissant. He looked at Christy and smiled. "Hey, tell your uncle thanks for me. These are good."

Christy reached for a paper towel and gently wiped the side of Todd's mouth. "You had some jelly right there," she explained. Then she immediately felt self-conscious. *Why am I wiping his mouth like he's my baby brother? Did that bother him?*

"Thanks," Todd said. Then he looked at her as she never remembered him looking at her before. It was a strong, deep, intense look that shot through her and ignited every memory she had of Todd. Every emotion. In that instant, she realized this was really Todd. They were really back together on the beach. This was the morning she had dreamed about for weeks, and her dream was coming true.

CHAPTER FOUR

The Way to a Man's Heart

It seems that when dreams come true, they never turn out the same way you dreamed them. They twist and turn and disappoint, leaving you wanting so much more. I don't know which to blame: the dream itself or the reality that dissolves the dream.

That's how Christy began her journal entry on Christmas night, snuggled under her warm covers in the privacy of "her" room.

The morning on the beach hadn't exactly turned out the way she thought it would. It had gone too fast. They ate, and Todd talked some about his mom's wedding. But right when Christy was finally beginning to feel at ease and enjoy their time together, Todd had jumped up, announced he had promised Shawn's parents he would be at their house at 9:00, and left. No big goodbye. No hug. Absolutely no hint of when he would call her or see her again.

Christy knew Todd and Shawn had been close friends for years, but Shawn had died last summer. Why was Todd leaving her to go spend the day with Shawn's parents? It didn't make sense.

She wrote in her diary how she had felt sitting alone by the dwindling fire and watching Todd walk away, his arms full of gear. He didn't even look back. Their dream breakfast was over, and she felt abandoned. Forsaken.

She probably would have stayed there, shivering in the morning chill, feeling sorry for herself, if it hadn't been for her soaked brother's whines to go back to the house. Gathering her things, she had trudged through the sand, miserable and cranky. Behind her, only the fire remained, burning into ashes.

Back at the house, her parents asked about "the crazy breakfast." Christy joined them at the kitchen table and began by apologizing for not being up-front about the situation. Marti kept interjecting her approving comments about Todd, and David joined her, giving full details of how Todd had taught him to skim-board.

"Sounds like a boy we'd like to meet someday," Mom said.

"But remember, Christy, you're not allowed to date until you're 16," Dad said. "We don't mind if you spend time with Todd and your other friends this week, as long as you're not going on a date." His tone was gruff; then he added, "Don't ever lie to your mother and me. If you want more freedom and privileges, then you show us you're trustworthy."

"She is," Bob interjected quickly.

"We want to trust you, Christy," Dad said a bit more gently, "but trust is something you earn by making wise choices and by being honest."

Christy felt humiliated, having everyone looking on as her dad lectured her.

"If we didn't trust you, Christy, we wouldn't let you stay here this week," her mom added. "Just don't take advantage of the privilege, all right?"

Christy nodded. Her stomach felt awful. She had so many things she wanted to say, like, "You can trust me. I've made a lot of wise choices you don't even know about. I'm really trying hard, even though I slip up every now and then." But all she did was force a smile and nod.

Mom smiled. Marti smiled. Bob smiled. Nobody said anything. They just smiled tight, forced smiles.

"Well," Christy said, excusing herself, "thanks for letting David and me stay this week. You can trust me. I'll do my best."

"We know you will, honey," her dad said.

Christy slipped out of the room and changed into sweats. She knew her dad was right about needing to be honest and trustworthy, and she knew she deserved the lecture. Still, it made her feel small and shaken, stripped of what little magic the morning had held.

Now, at day's end, trying to write all these feelings out, she felt even more dismal. She knew she couldn't mess things up this week. But somehow, without getting around her parents' directive, she had to spend as much time as she could with Todd. They said she could see him, just not go out with him.

She would have to plan a bunch of group things, then. Get all the gang from the summer back together so she could be with Todd.

Her final entry in her diary read:

This week, I've got to find out where I stand with Todd. I need to know where our relationship is and where it's going.

She had his phone number. Turning out the light, Christy determined that if he didn't call by noon tomorrow, she would call him, and she would have something planned for them to do.

The phone rang at exactly 11:45 the next day. But it was Tracy, not Todd. At first Christy acted frustrated that Tracy had called right then, but then she caught herself.

This was Tracy, her friend! And she really wanted to spend time with Tracy, too. Tracy was close friends with Todd. They could all do something together. She quickly changed her tone of voice and invited Tracy over to make cookies.

Right when she hung up, Marti came swishing down the stairs, dressed in navy blue pants, a white blouse, and a navy blue, V-neck sweater with some kind of emblem on the pocket. She looked cute—like a schoolgirl in a new uniform.

"Ready, Christy?"

"Ready for what?"

"Why, shopping, dear. I thought we'd go shopping. We're getting an awfully late start. If you want to wear what you have on, it's all right." Marti reached for her purse on the front hall tree and turned to look at Christy over her shoulder. "Well, come along, Christy. Don't just stand there."

Christy took a deep breath and two steps forward. She was taller than her aunt, and at this moment, even that tiny bit of leverage helped give her courage.

"You know what, Aunt Marti? I didn't know we were supposed to go shopping. Did you mention it to me earlier?"

"I suppose not. But everyone goes shopping right after—"

Christy gently interrupted. "Since I didn't know your plans, I made my own plans. I invited Tracy over to bake cookies. Uncle Bob said it was okay."

Marti looked stunned. She stammered, "Well, then, I . . ."

"I didn't mean to mess up your plans. It's just that you didn't tell me."

"I see. Yes, I understand," Marti stated, pursing her lips. With a brisk turn of her head, she called into the den, where the TV blared. "David! David, come here, dear."

"What is it?" David called back without moving.

"David, I want you to turn off that television and come here, darling."

"David," Christy yelled above her aunt's controlled voice.

"Do what Aunt Marti says—now!"

"Okay, okay!" David, wearing sweatpants and a skateboard T-shirt, appeared in the entryway. He scrunched up his nose and squinted through his glasses. "What?"

"David, we're going shopping. Now. You need to comb your hair and get your shoes on." Marti looked awfully smug.

"Aw, do I have to go?"

"Yes!" Christy stated sternly, yet inwardly suppressing a laugh. She didn't know who would drive whom nuts first, Marti or David. This would be a shopping trip to remember.

Within five minutes, they were out the door, David already begging Marti to take him to McDonald's for lunch.

Bob helped Christy find what she needed in the kitchen. It really amazed her. At home they never had this much food in the refrigerator at one time. Their cupboards never held so much nor such a variety. Bob even had different kinds of chocolate chips, including white chocolate. These cookies were going to be gourmet!

Tracy arrived and handed Christy a plate of fudge. "This is for you. My mom and I make fudge every year. I hope you like it."

"Are you kidding? I love anything chocolate. Thanks, Tracy. But now I feel bad that I don't have something for you."

Bob's voice came from the den. "Do you like cheese, Tracy?"

"Pardon me?" Tracy called back.

"Never mind," Christy said, laughing and steering Tracy away from her crazy uncle and into the kitchen. "Come on. Let's make some cookies. We have enough ingredients to make a couple of batches. I thought maybe we could take some to some people this afternoon, if they turn out well."

Petite Tracy, her shoulder-length brown hair pulled back in a ponytail, smiled a knowing smile. "You mean, maybe we could take some to Todd?"

Christy blushed. "Yes. And everybody else, too. Heather and Doug, and you know, all the guys from this summer."

Tracy placed her hand on Christy's arm and, with a teasing look on her face, said, "You don't have to explain, Christy. I know who you mean. And yes, I think Todd would really appreciate it."

They both giggled.

"Is there anybody in particular you'd like to deliver a box of cookies to?" Christy probed, curious if Tracy had her heart set on any certain guy.

"Well, actually . . . " Tracy didn't look up as she hesitated; then she said, "I'm sort of interested in somebody, but I don't think he's interested in me."

"Who?"

"I don't want to say. I'd feel horrible if everybody knew that I liked him, especially if he's not interested in me."

"Oh, come on! Tell me!"

"I'll tell you this week if he acts at all interested in me. Otherwise, I'm going to give up on him."

"You'd better tell me."

"I will. I promise. Only if it looks like there's any hope, okay?"

"Okay."

The girls shook hands on it and set to work.

Bob had a great kitchen for cooking: plenty of counter space and every possible size of measuring cup and mixing bowl. They started with a huge mixing bowl and doubled Bob's own recipe for gourmet chocolate-chip cookies, using real butter and mixing it with brown and white sugar until it looked like caramel pudding. Next came eggs, flour, baking soda, and then the chocolate chips.

"Which kind should we put in?" Christy asked, snitching some white chocolate chips and popping them into her mouth.

"How about both?" Tracy said, pouring both bags of chips into the bowl.

Christy laughed and grabbed a scoop of dough. "These are going to be so good!"

They worked together, nibbling on the dough, then placing rounded balls on the cookie sheets.

"Do you want anything to drink?" Christy asked, looking in the refrigerator.

"Do they have any diet drinks?"

Christy turned around and burst into laughter.

"What's so funny?" Tracy asked, popping another ball of cookie dough into her mouth.

"I just think it's funny that we've eaten about 10,000 calories in cookie dough, and you ask for a diet drink."

Tracy laughed and washed the dough off her hands. "Never mind. I'll just have some water. I feel kind of sick to my stomach from all this dough."

"Me, too. Let's get these two cookie trays going so we can take them to Todd's. You put them in the oven, and I'll find a couple of boxes to put them in," Christy said.

She set to work, lining two nice boxes with tissue paper. Within half an hour, the boxes were filled with warm, soft, delicious cookies.

"Should we take these over now?" Christy hoped Tracy wouldn't think she was being pushy or acting as if she didn't want to be with Tracy but only wanted to be with Todd.

"Sure," Tracy agreed without hesitation. "We can freeze the rest of this dough. That's what my mom always does. We'd better clean the kitchen up, though."

"I'll do the dishes," Christy volunteered. "Do you want to get your box of cookies ready for your mystery boyfriend? Now, what was his name . . . ?"

"Christy, Christy!" Tracy said in a mock scolding voice. "I told you, I'd only tell if he showed interest in me on his own. I don't like it when it turns into a game and everybody except the guy knows you like him. Then all your friends go up to him and say, 'Guess what? Tracy likes you!' And then the poor guy has to decide if he's going to break your heart or play along with the game. I don't want to play that game with—" She caught herself.

"With . . . ?" Christy prodded.

Tracy covered her mouth with her hand. "I can't believe it! I almost said his name, didn't I!"

"Your secret would have been safe with me."

"I know it would, Christy. But haven't you ever been caught in the middle of a relationship, and you suddenly look at it for what it really is, and you say, 'Wait a minute! This is everyone else's idea, not mine'? And you wish you could start all over and just be friends for a while without all the pressure everyone else puts on you to be boyfriend and girlfriend?"

Christy pulled up a stool and sat down. "Tracy, I know exactly what you mean. There's this guy at school, Rick, and I don't know if I really like him or if I just like him because everyone keeps saying, 'Oh, Rick asked about you today. He likes you—we can tell.' So, yes, I know exactly what you mean, and I won't bug you anymore."

"Do you like Rick?"

"Yes and no. It's not the same as it is with Todd. Like yesterday. Nothing turned out the way I thought it would when we made breakfast on the beach. Todd left without saying if he'd call or anything. I felt depressed about it, but I didn't worry about whether or not Todd liked me anymore. I feel that the next time I see him, we'll just pick up where we left off."

"Todd has that way about him, doesn't he? He has to be the most loyal guy in the world," Tracy agreed. "Once you're his friend, you're always his friend."

"Exactly! But it's not that way with Rick at all. When I came up here a couple of days ago, he wasn't speaking to me. I can't even guess what things will be like when I see him again."

"Don't you hate that!"

"Yes!"

Tracy pulled the last cookie sheet from the oven and turned it off. "And that's why, even though I like this one guy a lot, I'm going to wait for him to show some interest in me, unprompted by all my well-meaning friends."

"You're a good influence on me, Tracy," Christy said as she returned to the sink and finished loading the dishwasher. "I don't know if I ever thanked you for the Bible you and Todd gave me."

"You did. And speaking of Todd, I'm going to call him and make sure he's home," Tracy said.

"Good idea!" Christy couldn't wait to get going. "I'll be ready as soon as I brush my hair and tell my uncle where we're going."

Christy loved this feeling of independence, being able to bake cookies; talk so openly with Tracy, as if they'd been best friends all their lives; and now go over to Todd's house.

That last part seemed too good to be true. After five months of being thousands of miles apart and carrying on a one-sided correspondence with Todd, he was so nearby that she could simply walk over to his house and see him and talk to him and be close to him.

The painful part was that they had only a few days to be this close. Christy knew that every moment with Todd had to count.

CHAPTER FIVE

All-Time Friends

"Hold on a minute, girls," Uncle Bob called as they headed out the door. "Almost forgot. I've got something for Todd, too." Uncle Bob appeared at the door with a gift bag all tied up. "Have fun, ladies!"

"What is it?" Christy asked, shaking the bag.

Uncle Bob gave her one of his "twinkle-grins" and said, "A little something a guy like Todd might appreciate."

The afternoon was clear and warm, yet the brisk wind made Christy glad she had put on a sweatshirt. She wondered if Todd still wore the sweatshirt she got for him in San Francisco last summer. A bigger question was, will he like the T-shirt she painted for him?

"Did you get anything for Todd?" Christy asked Tracy.

"Yes, I usually buy him a present. This year I got him a CD. The new Debbie Stevens one. Do you have it?"

"No. I bought one, but I ended up giving it to Rick. I kind of wish I hadn't because I don't think he liked it."

"What did Rick give you?"

"A stupid book. It was a joke. Some guys have such a strange sense of humor."

Tracy laughed. "Don't I know it!"

"I have a T-shirt for Todd," Christy explained. "But I don't know if I should give it to him. I painted a surfer on it. I was going to give it to him yesterday, but I completely forgot about it. It was probably a good thing, because he didn't give me anything."

"Except the breakfast," Tracy reminded her. "I was pretty impressed when I heard he bought the food and set the whole thing up. That's a nice gift, if you ask me."

"You're right. I should be more grateful. It's just that the birds ate everything, and my little brother ended up spending more time with Todd than I did."

"Still, Christy. What girl wouldn't love for her boyfriend to go to all that trouble for her?"

"My boyfriend?"

"Well, you know, Todd's your friend, and he's a boy. I don't know what else to call him." Tracy led Christy around a corner and down the street to where Todd lived.

"You know what? I wish there was a word for something between 'just friends' and 'boyfriend.'"

"I know what you mean," Tracy said. "And there needs to be a word between 'like' and 'love,' too. Either you 'like' a guy or you're supposedly 'in love.' There's definitely a middle area, but there's no word for it."

"Then let's make up a word!"

Tracy laughed. "Should we ask Todd to help us? This is his house." She stopped in front of a narrow two-story house that faced the street, not the beach. From the outside, it looked smaller than Bob and Marti's, but newer.

"Merry day after Christmas!" Christy said brightly when Todd answered the door.

"Hey, how's it going?" Todd said, welcoming them into the messiest living room Christy had ever seen. Newspapers, dirty dishes, and clothes were all over the place. The most obvious thing to her, though, was the absence of any Christmas decorations. No tree, no wreaths. No evidence that a family lived here or had celebrated Christmas.

"Sorry it's such a mess," Todd apologized, clearing a place for them to sit on the couch. "The housekeeper hasn't come yet this week. My dad's in Switzerland."

"Switzerland?" Christy said in surprise.

"How long has he been gone?" Tracy asked.

"Four or five days. I think he gets back on Saturday."

"Todd!" Tracy looked as distressed as Christy felt. "What did you do for Christmas?"

He turned to Christy and smiled. "Had breakfast on the beach and then hung out at Shawn's."

Tracy hesitated and then said, "I bet they appreciated your being there." She held out her bag full of gifts.

Christy followed, handing him her bag and saying, "Merry Christmas from us a day late, or a year early, whichever you prefer. Go ahead! Open your presents!"

Todd sat down and gathered the boxes on his lap. He opened Bob's gift bag first. Christy groaned when Todd pulled out a handful of international cheese triangles.

"Cool!" Todd said. "Is this the same kind we had for breakfast?"

"Who knows," Christy said, shaking her head. "We have such a variety of cheeses to choose from! My uncle sent them over. I didn't know what he put in the bag. Open the box. I know you'll like what's in there."

"Oh, man!" Todd exclaimed, pulling off the lid and grabbing a soft cookie. "Did you make these?"

"Tracy and I did. Just this afternoon. Do you like them?"

Todd scarfed down two before answering with a garbled, "Definitely!"

"Now try the fudge!" Tracy opened her box, and Todd complied, stuffing the biggest piece into his mouth.

The girls laughed as he tried to swallow and compliment Tracy on the fudge at the same time.

He opened the CD next and said, "Thanks, Trace. You don't know how much I appreciate this."

"One more," Tracy said, handing him Christy's box.

Christy felt queasy. Would he like it? Would he ever wear it? Should she have given him a CD, too, like Tracy had?

"Cool!" Todd held up the shirt, and Tracy added her oohs and aahs.

"Do you really like it?" Christy asked.

"Definitely!" Todd said, giving her a deep, warm look.

"That is really good, Christy," Tracy said. "She painted it herself, Todd. Did you know that?"

"No way! Really?"

Christy felt her cheeks turning red. She nodded, feeling relieved that he really seemed to like it.

Todd stood up, stepped over a pile of newspapers, and gave Christy a hug around the neck, and then gave Tracy the same. "Thanks, Christy. Thanks, Tracy."

He snatched up another cookie and headed for the kitchen. "Either of you want something to drink? We've got cranberry juice and 7-Up."

"Got milk?" Tracy asked with a laugh.

Todd stuck his head back into the living room with a grin on his face. "Nope. Drank the last of it this morning."

"Then I'll have 7-Up," Tracy called to him.

"Me too," Christy echoed.

"I have a strong urge to find the vacuum cleaner and go to work on this place," Tracy whispered while Todd was still in the kitchen. "It's such a mess."

For the first time ever, Christy felt sorry for Todd, and it surprised her. For so long he had made her feel all kinds of emotions, but she had never pitied him. Now seeing him in this messy, expensively decorated house and knowing he had been all alone for Christmas made her heart ache for him. How could his parents abandon him like that? And on Christmas?

Perhaps their breakfast on the beach had been a dream for him as well. She was seeing a whole new side of Todd, and she wanted so badly to tell him how deeply she cared for him.

"Can I put the CD on?" Tracy asked when Todd stepped back into the living room.

"Sure."

Tracy turned on the elaborate stereo and took out the CD that was already in the CD player. She looked at it before putting the new Debbie Stevens CD in and then yelled, "Todd! Why didn't you tell me you already had this CD?"

"It's cool," he said, handing Christy a can of 7-Up. "I'll keep one in the house and one in Gus the Bus."

"Did you put a CD player in Gus?" Tracy asked.

"No, but I plan to. One day."

"Well, Todd, if you hadn't taken the cellophane off, I could have taken it back and bought you something else. A different CD or something."

Todd stood next to Christy and said, "It's a Christmas present from you, Tracy. I would never take back anything one of my all-time friends gave me."

"Now that's good," Tracy said, turning to Christy. " 'All-time friends.' What do you think of that?"

Christy thought a moment. "It's all right, but not exactly it."

"Not exactly what?" Todd asked, plopping down next to her on the couch.

"On the way over we were trying to think of an expression for whatever it is that comes between 'like' and 'love' or between 'just friends' and 'in love.' Got anything better than 'all-time friends'?"

"Not me. I'm not the writer in this group. You are, Christy."

Christy put up her hands as if defending herself. "I don't have any great ideas."

"We'll have to work on that one," Tracy suggested. "And you know what else I'd like to do this week while we're all together? I'd like to talk about stuff in the Bible. You know, maybe everyone can read the same thing and then talk about it when we get together."

Todd and Christy both looked at her as if they weren't sure what to make of her suggestion.

"What do you want us to read?" Todd asked.

"How about Philippians? Or First John? Or some of the Psalms?"

"First John sounds good," Todd said.

"All right, good." Tracy looked pleased with herself.

"Do you want to do something tomorrow?" Christy blurted out. Todd and Tracy both looked at her, waiting for her to go on.

"I mean, you guys could come over, or we could all go do something together."

"Sure," Todd said without hesitating. "What do you want to do?"

"We could go to the movies," Tracy suggested. "That is, if there's anything worth seeing. Or we could rent a video and watch it at my house."

"Do you guys ever go ice-skating?" Christy asked. She had ice-skated every winter since she could remember, outside on the frozen pond with all her friends. California had to have indoor rinks somewhere where they could all go.

"That sounds like fun!" Tracy said. "Let's get everybody together and go tomorrow to that rink in Costa Mesa. If we all pitch in for gas, will you drive, Todd?''

"Sure. When do you want to go?''

"I don't know. About 1:00 or 2:00. We could all meet at my house," Tracy said. "Let's meet around noon for lunch. My mom won't mind. Then we could all leave from there.''

"Sounds cool. What time is it now?" Todd asked.

Tracy looked at her watch. "Oh, no, Christy! It's almost 5:00.''

"I have to go, too," Todd said. "I'm going over to Doug's. I'll tell him about ice-skating tomorrow.''

"Could I go with you to Doug's?" Tracy asked.

"Sure. Come on, Christy. I'll drop you off on the way.''

They all hopped into Todd's old VW van, "Gus the Bus." Both girls squeezed into the front seat, with Christy closest to Todd. Christy couldn't help but smile to herself with memories of last summer when more than once Christy had been jealous of Tracy because Tracy had been the one sitting in the front seat and Christy had been in the back. Now they were sharing the seat and sharing their friendship with Todd. The three of them really, truly were "all-time friends" together. It was a wonderful thing to Christy, and it made her feel good deep inside.

When Todd pulled up in front of Bob and Marti's, he thanked Christy again for the shirt and cookies.

"I'm glad you like them," Christy said. She wanted to reach over and hug him and tell him she was sorry he'd been alone for most of Christmas. She wanted to whisper in his ear that she couldn't wait to see him again tomorrow. But all she did was smile and look into his clear blue eyes and say, "Thanks for the ride.''

Todd tilted his chin back, gave her his usual, "Later," and then drove off with Tracy.

Christy stood on the curb and waved good-bye to her two "all-

time friends." When she turned to walk back into Bob and
Marti's house, her heart was full of anticipation. So what if her
breakfast with Todd hadn't been all that special? Tomorrow they
would go ice-skating, and he would hold her hand. He'd have to.
It's very natural for people to hold hands when they skate. She
knew how wonderful it felt to slip her hand into his. Even though
it had been months, she remembered exactly what Todd's hand
felt like. Tomorrow she'd feel it again: strong and warm and wonderful.

Smiling widely to herself, Christy opened the front door and
stepped inside. *Todd and I really, truly are more than "in like." I just
know it. Maybe we're even on our way to "in love."*

CHAPTER SIX

Skating Along

That evening at the dinner table, David squished his green beans with his fork and gave his opinion of shopping with Aunt Marti.

"She made me buy a pink shirt, Christy. Pink!" He scrunched up his nose in his favorite hamster look.

"David looks very good in muted colors. It isn't really pink. I'd say it was a light mauve tone," Aunt Marti said.

"It's pink," David muttered. "And the McDonald's we went to didn't even have a playground."

"You're getting a little too old for playgrounds, don't you think, dear?" Aunt Marti's smoothly made-up face seemed to twitch just a bit. Christy wondered how awful the experience had actually been. Who had been the most ornery—Marti or David?

"I know a playground down at Balboa for big kids," Uncle Bob said. "Why don't we go there tomorrow, David? If I can still play there, so can you."

David nodded and smiled, his mouth full of baked potato. It wasn't a pretty sight.

"Then Christy and I will spend the day shopping," Aunt Marti stated.

"I kind of already made some plans for tomorrow," Christy

said slowly. "Tracy invited me over to her house at noon, and then a bunch of us are going ice-skating. Todd said he would drive. Would that be okay?"

"Sounds like fun," Uncle Bob said.

Aunt Marti put down her fork with an exaggerated thump. "I'm surprised, Christina, at how quickly you've managed to fill up your social calendar this week. Do you suppose you'll have any time to fit us into your plans?"

"We just decided today, Aunt Marti. I didn't know you had anything else planned!" *There was a time, dear Aunt, when you pushed me out on the beach to make these new friends. Do you now object to my spending time with them?*

In a squeezed voice, Aunt Marti said, "Tell me, dear, are you available, say, the day after tomorrow? Perhaps we could go to lunch."

Christy glanced at Uncle Bob and then answered in a voice that came out too sweet, too bright: "Sure! That would be great."

Satisfied, Aunt Marti smiled, looked at her food, and slowly took another bite.

All Christy could think about was, *A whole day. I'm going to end up spending a whole day with my aunt, and I could have been spending it with Todd.*

When Aunt Marti dropped Christy off at Tracy's house the next day, she said, "Now remember, we've got plans for tomorrow, so please don't promise any of your friends that you'll do something with them. All right?"

Christy agreed and thanked her aunt for the ride, but inside she felt soured. Her aunt had manipulated her all last summer, but now it irritated her to pieces. She no longer welcomed Aunt Marti's interference in her life.

Nevertheless, her dad had said she was to remember that she was a guest this week, and she was to fit into her aunt and uncle's plans. She would simply have to try harder.

Heather and Leslie opened the door and warmly greeted Christy. She stepped into the living room, where two guys were planted in front of the TV, playing a video game.

She could see Todd in the kitchen, helping Tracy and her mom make pizza. He sprinkled a handful of cheese onto the top before shoving another handful of cheese into his mouth. Tracy playfully punched him in the arm. Christy wondered if she should go into the kitchen or wait until Todd noticed her.

"Christy!" Doug suddenly stood in front of her. He had changed a lot since the summer. Home for Christmas vacation after his first semester at San Diego State, he looked like a college student. His blond hair was styled short on the sides and longer in front. He wore a neatly pressed green shirt and was clean-shaven. The only thing that hadn't changed was the little boy look in his eyes when he grinned.

"Hi, Doug!"

"How are you?" He gave her an awkward hug around the neck and said, "Come over here and sit down. Tell me about Escondido. How's school? Do you like it better here than in Wisconsin?"

They chatted easily for a few minutes, with Doug turned sideways, resting his arm on the back of the couch. "You look good in blue," he said. "Makes your eyes look real clear."

Christy could feel herself blushing as she said, "Thanks."

Just then Todd walked into the living room. Christy caught a glimpse of him out of the corner of her eye. Was he coming over to talk to her? No, he went back into the kitchen.

Doug talked about school and his new truck. Then, out of nowhere, he said, "You know, Christy, I'm so glad you're here and that everything's going well for you!" He gave her another quick, awkward hug. It was a real "Doug" thing. He was always hugging people and trying to cheer them up and encourage them.

Just then, Tracy popped her head into the room. When her gaze fell on Doug and Christy, hugging on the couch, she gave them a strange look that lasted only an instant. Then she called out, "Come eat, you guys! Pizza's ready!"

They gathered in the kitchen around the counter, which was spread with soft drinks, paper plates, and three steaming pizzas. Doug reached over and snitched an olive. Christy playfully swatted his hand. She caught Tracy's gaze, and again, for a brief moment, Tracy looked mad.

"Let's pray, you guys," Brian suggested and took the hands of the people standing next to him around the counter.

The rest of them followed his gesture. Doug took Christy's hand as she reached for Heather's on the other side. Doug's hand felt strong, a little bit rough, but very warm.

The sensations confused her. They were supposed to be praying, like brothers and sisters, yet she felt a bombardment of mixed emotions.

I wish I were holding Todd's hand instead. Or do I? Doug is acting interested in me, but is he really? Why is Tracy looking mad? Was I supposed to help her make the pizza? And why is she over there, next to Todd, when that's where I want to be?

"Amen," Brian said. They dropped hands and dove for the pizza.

Christy felt ashamed that she hadn't heard a word of Brian's prayer. She slipped one slice of pizza onto her plate, grabbed a can of soda pop, and found a chair at the kitchen table next to Heather. She thought it would be good if she kept her distance from the guys for a few minutes, until she had her thoughts straight.

"Your hair looks cute," she said to Heather, who automatically patted the French braid Leslie had made.

"It feels as though it's about to fall out."

"Doesn't look like it," Christy said, examining the braid more closely.

"Your hair is long enough to braid," Heather commented. "I can't believe it grew so fast!"

"I like it long," said a male voice.

Christy turned to see Todd sitting down next to her.

"What?" Heather said in a squeaky voice. "You like Christy's hair long? When did you ever see it long?"

Todd took a bite of his pizza, the cheese stringing out. Doug reached over and broke the string bridge with his finger before sitting down across from Christy. She felt excited with the sudden attention, yet uncomfortable at the same time.

Todd swallowed his wad of pizza and looked right at Christy with an expression she didn't recognize. "Used to be almost to her waist," he said. "I liked it long." Then he took another bite of pizza.

Christy sat perfectly still, running the information through her mind. She came to California last summer with long hair but had it all whacked off the day before she met Todd. How would he know she used to have long hair?

"I liked it long, too," Doug added.

Just then Tracy came over to the table and took the last chair, right next to Doug.

"What are you guys talking about?" she asked.

"Tracy," Heather said, sounding perplexed, "did you ever see Christy with long hair? These guys are being mean and saying they liked her better with long hair."

The girls looked at Christy, waiting for her to make sense of the conversation. The guys kept eating, glancing at each other as if they knew some great secret.

Christy quickly pulled an explanation together. "I had long

hair the first few days I was here last summer, but I got it cut the day before I met all of you. I don't know when these guys saw it long, unless . . . " She stopped. "Oh, no. Were you the guys who made fun of my old bathing suit that day on the beach?" Christy looked at them with panic in her eyes.

"What bathing suit?" Tracy asked.

"What day?" Heather said. "What are you talking about?"

Doug and Todd kept eating, wearing their smirky little expressions. Christy looked as though she was about to throw something at them.

Doug must have realized her intentions because he quickly swallowed, leaned forward, and said, "We weren't the ones who made the rude comments. But we did notice you that day."

There was a pause, and then Doug added, "We definitely noticed you that day."

"You were kind of hard to miss," Todd mumbled, before stuffing another bite of pizza past his upturned lips.

Doug nearly choked on his drink when Todd said it. He grabbed a napkin, covered his mouth and nose, and sputtered, "Rude, Todd! Rude!"

Christy wanted to run from the room and cry her eyes out. How could they do this to her? That was a horrible experience, the day the surfers laughed at her "green bean" bathing suit. Why would Todd and Doug be so mean as to bring it up now? She lowered her head and blinked fast so the tears wouldn't come.

"Anybody else want some more pizza?" Todd said, getting up from his chair. Then, before he left the table, he leaned over and whispered in Christy's ear so no one else could hear, "I like your hair now, but I really liked it long." Then off he went to get more pizza.

Christy's heart pounded. She could still feel the sensation of his whisper, his warm breath on her neck. The welled-up tears instantly evaporated, but then the anger came. *Why do you always do this to me, Todd?* she thought. *You put me on this roller coaster, and the worst part is, you seem to enjoy it!*

Skinny Heather turned red in the face and pounded her hand on the table. "You guys are all a bunch of . . . you're all . . ."

"Gweeks?" Doug questioned and let out a hearty laugh.

Todd returned laughing, too, looking as if he were having a great time.

"Well, maybe we girls just don't want to go ice-skating with all you 'gweeks.' What do you think, Tracy, Christy, should we leave these guys and go to the mall?"

"No!" Tracy said too quickly, and they all looked at her in surprise. "I mean, I already called the ice rink, and they're giving us a discount because we have more than eight people coming."

"We should make the guys go by themselves and pay the higher price," Heather said and then gave Todd and Doug a playful smirk. For emphasis, she quickly stuck out her tongue at them.

"I wouldn't keep a dirty thing like that in my mouth either," Doug said.

Todd joined him in another boom of laughter. They were like that all the way to the ice-skating rink—like two eight-year-olds full of little boy tricks and jokes. It drove Christy crazy. She confided her frustration to Heather as they sat on a bench, watching the group skate to the blaring music.

"Todd is driving me crazy! He's acting like such a brat. I'm almost expecting him to pull a frog out of his pocket and chase me around the parking lot!"

"Do you really like him?" Heather asked. Wisps of her thin blond hair had come out of the braid and now danced around her face. She looked so innocent, so trustworthy.

"Can I tell you something?" Christy asked, lowering her voice.

"Of course." Heather's eyes grew wide in anticipation.

"I really, really, really like Todd. But I can't figure out where I stand with him. One day he acts as if he likes me; the next day he's a brat."

"That's because he doesn't know how much you like him! You're so cute and sweet and friendly with everybody, I bet he has no idea that you're really interested in him more than, say, Doug."

"That's the crazy part," Christy confided. "I almost thought he was jealous at Tracy's because I was talking to Doug. But then he and Doug said all that embarrassing stuff, and I could have slugged both of them."

"You should have!" Heather said. "You know, I think that might be the way to go."

"What, physical abuse?"

"No." Heather giggled. "Get Todd jealous. He's not a real fast mover, you know."

"Yes, I know."

"So, motivate him. Flirt your face off with Doug, and Todd will see that he's going to lose you if he doesn't act quickly."

"I don't know, Heather. I'm not sure playing games is the way to go—with any guy."

"Just try it. What have you got to lose? Go ask Doug to skate and see what happens."

Christy shook her head hesitantly.

"What have you got to lose? Come on, Christy. Try it. Go!"

Christy reluctantly pegged her way across the floor on her ice skates and stood by the rail, watching the blur of people skating by. She saw Todd slowly skating on the outside with two junior high girls fluttering nearby, ready to pounce whenever he tumbled, which was quite often. Todd might be the tall, handsome champion surfer, but he was a klutz on ice skates. Christy figured it must be a different set of muscles or a different sense of balance. Whatever it was, she had it and Todd definitely did not. The junior high girls spotted him the minute he came in and had followed him around the rink all afternoon.

Christy smiled, remembering when she and Paula, her old best friend in Wisconsin, were that age. They used to hover around the cute older guys, dreaming big high school dreams and exaggerating the stories about the guys each time they retold them.

Now Christy was a big high-schooler. Was she still playing games? Was Heather's "make-him-jealous" idea as stupid as some of the ideas Christy and Paula had schemed up in junior high?

Just then the music stopped, the skaters cleared the ice, and the lights dimmed. The disc jockey announced a couples' skate.

Christy wished she were stepping out on the ice at this moment with Todd holding her hand, the way she had dreamed the day before.

"There you are," Doug said, suddenly coming up behind her. "I was looking for you. Want to skate?"

"I, well . . . " Christy hated it when she stammered like this. She didn't want to play a game to make Todd jealous, yet Doug had asked her, not the other way around. She glanced back at Heather, who was urging her with a wide-eyed expression to move forward.

"Come on!" Doug said, taking her by the hand. "You know how to skate, Christy. I saw you out there. Don't act like you don't."

Doug knew how to skate, too. Forward, backward—she had even seen him do a halfway decent spin in the center of the floor earlier. Now they skated hand-in-hand around the dimly lit rink. They were smooth.

Doug said, "Let's try something." He pulled around in front

of her so that he was skating backward. He put his hands on her waist, and she put hers on his upper arms. "You tell me if I'm going to crash, okay?"

"I hope you've done this before," Christy said tensely, "because I can only skate forward."

"No way! You can skate backward, can't you?"

"Look out!" Christy cautioned.

Doug glanced over his shoulder and barely missed two little kids who had just tumbled. "Close one! Good call! Here, I'll teach you how to skate backward."

For the rest of the couples' skate, Doug and Christy worked on their little routine. First Doug skated backward, then he would gently spin Christy around so she was going backward. At first she kept looking over her shoulder, but then she relaxed and had a great time, feeling like a ballet dancer gracefully slicing through the air. It was wonderful.

She looked for Todd but didn't see him. Was he watching her? What was he thinking?

The soft music came to an end, and the lights went back up. The floor flooded with noisy skaters. Doug directed Christy to the center of the rink to work out a spin in which Doug would twirl Christy around and she would end up in his other arm. It was so much fun, Christy barely noticed when the lights dimmed again, and "triples" were announced.

"Let's get another person so we can keep skating," Doug said. "There's Heather."

He pointed to a waving Heather at the sidelines and motioned for her to come out on the ice to join them. Heather grabbed Doug's free hand, and the three took off around the rink.

When Doug wasn't looking, Heather motioned to Christy as if to say, "Good work! You're flirting with Doug just the way I told you to!"

Christy was quiet. She had forgotten all about trying to make Todd jealous. She and Doug were just having fun. It was no big deal. She didn't even feel all that tingly about him holding her hand anymore. As a matter of fact, his hands were kind of sweaty.

"Look!" Heather squeaked and pointed to a threesome bumbling along in front of them.

It was Todd and two of the adoring junior-highers.

"Hey, dude," Doug called as they skimmed past, "nice crutches."

The girls giggled and tugged on Todd's arms, pulling him along. Todd looked absolutely miserable. Christy felt guilty and jealous. Guilty for being with Doug, and crazy as it sounded, jealous of the junior high girls. What were those little squirts doing with her "boyfriend," anyway?

This was not the way she had hoped the day would be. It had to get better. It had to change back into the dream she'd imagined the day before, where Todd was the one making her feel like a floating angel, and not Doug. This was not at all turning out the way Christy wanted it to. She had to talk to Todd.

CHAPTER SEVEN

The Hurt Puppy

Around 5:30 the group members turned in their skates and piled into Todd's van. A discussion ensued as to what they should do next—all go home, or go to dinner, or go to a movie and have popcorn and M&M's for dinner.

Christy felt like going home and starting the day over. She had spent the whole time at the ice rink with Doug and hadn't said one word to Todd. Sitting now in the front seat of Gus, she realized that this was the closest she had been to Todd all day. He looked okay—not mad or miserable but not great. Just okay.

The group voted on going to dinner at Richie's. Todd started up Gus and chugged out of the parking lot.

"I'd better call my aunt and uncle to make sure it's okay," Christy said softly.

Without turning to look at her, Todd, in his matter-of-fact way, said, "It's on the way. We'll stop by. If they say no, you're already home."

What's that supposed to mean? Christy thought. *That you don't want me to go? Are you hoping they'll say no so you can drop me off and be rid of me? Todd! I've waited months to see you, and now I can't even talk to you!*

When they pulled up in front of the house, Doug called after her, "Bring back some of those cookies you and Tracy made."

Christy hurried into the house and called out, "Uncle Bob?"

"In here," he answered from the den, where he sat with his feet up, reading the paper. The TV was on, and David was half watching it and half tinkering with his remote-control car.

"Everybody's out front waiting. They want to go to some place called Richie's for dinner. May I go with them?"

"Richie's, you say? Good choice. Sure. Here," he said, reaching into his pocket. "I've only got $50. Think that'll be enough?"

"Oh, that's too much. I only need $8 or $10, I think."

"Take the $50. Treat your friends to my favorite at Richie's: Oreo Fantasy shake. It's a killer. Have fun!"

"Where's she going?" David called out as Christy dashed out the door.

She jumped into Gus with renewed vigor. "My uncle gave me 50 bucks and told me to treat everybody to some kind of Oreo shake."

Only Todd heard her. Everyone else was wrapped up in various conversations, and Heather was laughing loudly in the backseat.

"Cool," was all Todd said without looking at her.

Come on, Todd! she thought, annoyed. *Talk to me! What's wrong?*

Just then Doug leaned forward, his head between Christy and Todd, and said, "Where are the cookies?"

"There weren't any left."

"Those were great cookies," Doug said. "Didn't you think so, Todd?"

Todd nodded but didn't say anything.

Now Christy was getting mad. Why was he acting like such a baby?

"So," Doug continued, apparently not bothered by the tension that seemed to hang between Todd and Christy, "when do you want to go skating again, Christy? We were getting pretty good out there. Did you see us, Todd? What do you think? Not bad, huh?"

Todd's words came out slowly and deliberately. "You're good, Doug. You two looked real good together."

Christy had heard those words before. That same phrase had run through her mind a dozen times last night, when she had dreamed about what it would be like to skate hand-in-hand with Todd, not with Doug! Todd wasn't supposed to say that. Somebody else was supposed to say that about her and Todd. Everything was turned around.

Todd pulled into a parking place next to the pier. The group tumbled out of the van, talking and laughing.

Doug opened Christy's door. "You coming?" he asked.

She climbed out and joined the gang marching down the pier. Todd led the pack, and Tracy was with Brian and Heather. Doug stayed right beside Christy.

The wind off the ocean whipped around them from every angle, chilling Christy to the bone. Diehard fishermen in down jackets lined the pier, their fishing poles jutting into the dark waters below. The crashing surf sprayed the air with a fine mist. Christy hugged herself, rubbing her arms to get warm.

"You cold?" Doug asked. Before she could answer, he slipped his jacket around her and left his arm around her shoulder, drawing her to his side.

Wait a minute! she thought. *Why is Doug doing this? What if somebody sees him? What if Todd sees him?*

She pulled away slightly, scanning the group ahead of them to see if anyone had noticed. They all still had their backs to them. Then, as if Doug could read her thoughts, he slipped his arm down. Funny. While they were ice-skating, it didn't bother her that he held her hand or put his arm around her. Now it felt uncomfortable. She didn't know if he was doing it in a brotherly way because she was so cold, or if he was acting as if they were a couple now.

What is wrong with me? Christy thought. *How come I'm so confused? First with Rick and now with Doug. And the only one I want to put his arm around me is Todd! But he won't even look at me.*

Doug hopped ahead of her a few steps and opened the door to Richie's, a small, charming diner at the end of the pier. It was a cozy place—inviting and warm—and looked like a snack bar from a '50s movie with its red vinyl seats at the booths and a long bar with red stools.

The group huddled together, waiting until the large corner booth opened up so they could all squeeze in. Christy hung back, hoping to arrange it so that she could sit by Todd. But Todd had already seated himself at the far end of the booth, with no room next to him.

Christy decided it was time to make her feelings known to Todd. He was the one she wanted to be with. She bravely walked over to his end of the booth, anticipating that he would scoot over or somehow make room for her. But he ignored her. She couldn't believe it. He totally ignored her.

"Christy," Doug called, "there's a place down here."

Fine! Christy thought angrily. *I'll go sit by you, Doug, and I'll laugh and have a good time and forget that Todd is even here.*

Tracy appeared at the booth and sized up the seating arrangement. She must have slipped into the rest room while they were playing musical chairs, because she had taken her hair out of its usual ponytail and now it cascaded to her shoulders, smooth and pretty. Grabbing a chair, she planted it on the end, right next to Doug. Doug stepped away from the booth and let Christy slide in next to him so that he was on the end and between Tracy and Christy.

Tracy gave Christy a rude glare and said, "Nice jacket."

"It's Doug's," Christy said defensively. "It was freezing out there."

"I know," Tracy said with an icy edge to her voice.

I can't believe this is happening! Christy thought. *These are all my perfect, ideal, Christian friends, and they're ready to kill me. What's wrong with everybody?* Christy opened a menu and stared at it without seeing the words.

"Chili fries sound great tonight!" Doug said energetically.

"Those are so gross," Leslie said.

"Hey, Todd," Doug yelled across the table, "what's that one you always get here?"

"Beach Burger," Todd said flatly, catching Christy's glance at the very moment she happened to look up. He held her gaze. Then he did something with his eyes. He didn't really move his eyes or eyebrows, or maybe he did just a tiny bit. It looked like in the old movies when the hero searched the maiden's face, scanning desperately for an answer. Or was he asking for an apology for not making room for her to sit by him?

Todd's look, his unspoken message, was too piercing. Christy turned away and hid behind her menu. All she could see were his screaming silver-blue eyes saying, "What are you doing to me, Christy?'"

Is he upset about how the day turned out, too? Christy thought hopefully. *Well, he certainly isn't doing much to change things!*

"And for you?" the waiter said, playfully tapping his pencil on Christy's menu. She looked up instantly and saw a guy in a white shirt with a black bow tie. He looked like a soda jerk out of *Happy Days.*

"Um, I guess I'll have a Beach Burger, and do you have Oreo shakes?"

"Oreo Fantasy," he said. "One of our specialties."

"I'll have one, then."

She sat quietly, watching Doug demonstrate to Tracy how to make a worm out of a paper straw wrapper. First he scrunched the wrapper real tight, like an accordion, and placed it on the table. Then, with the straw, he dripped water onto the "worm," and it grew instantly.

Tracy relaxed. "Is that what they teach you in college?" she teased, laughing and encouraging Doug's silly tricks.

Doug apparently loved it because he set to work on a magic trick with two quarters and a napkin.

Now Christy was the one left out, as Doug and Tracy worked to put his magic trick together. She thought Todd was looking at her, but when she casually glanced his way, he wasn't. She remained quiet while all the others chatted around her. Halfheartedly nibbling at her hamburger, she couldn't even enjoy the celebrated Oreo Fantasy shake.

While the others ate and talked, she slipped out and went into the tiny bathroom. Her reflection in the mirror surprised her. Her hair fuzzed all over from the damp air, and her cheeks and nose were still red from the ice-skating. Her eye shadow had turned into a blue-brown crease in the middle of her eyelid. Her mascara had left dark smudges in the bottom corners of both eyes.

She quickly dampened a paper towel and tried to fix her eye makeup. Then, half talking to God and half talking to herself, she said, "Did You see how everything got messed up today? Of course You did. Well, I don't mean to be rude or anything, but I don't think this is how Your other Christians are supposed to be acting toward me."

She paused, looked at her reflection, and added, "Not that I've been doing such a great job of being everybody's friend, but at least I'm not being outright rude like Tracy."

Just then the bathroom door lurched opened, and Heather

blew in breathlessly. "Christy, it's totally working! I can't believe this! I've never seen him act like this before."

"Who? Act like what?"

"Todd! He's acting like a hurt puppy. He's all mad at Doug. I can't believe how jealous he is!"

"But I don't want him to be jealous. I don't want him to be mad at anybody," Christy groaned. "Heather, it wasn't supposed to be like this."

"It wasn't?" Heather looked surprised.

"No! All this 'game' stuff doesn't work. Believe me."

"Of course it works. You skated with Doug, and Todd's jealous, isn't he?"

"Heather, I didn't skate with Doug to get Todd jealous, like you told me to. I ended up skating with Doug because we both could skate, that's all."

"Oh really? And the jacket?" Heather eyed Doug's jacket, which Christy still had on.

"I was cold, and Doug offered me his jacket."

Heather rolled her eyes and put her hand on her hip. "Christy, make up your mind whose game you're going to play, because it sure looks to me as though you're going after Doug."

"I'm not. Honest."

"Well, don't tell me. Tell Todd."

"I'd love to tell Todd. There's a whole bunch of things I'd love to tell Todd! Only he's not talking to me at the moment!" Christy felt herself getting angrier and angrier at Heather.

Heather shrugged her shoulders and looked at her hair in the mirror. "I guess you shouldn't have made him jealous, then."

Christy threw her head back and closed her eyes. "Heather!"

"What?"

"First you tell me to make Todd jealous, then when he is, and everybody is mad at me, you tell me I shouldn't have done it!"

"Well, how was I supposed to know? It seemed like a good idea. So what are you going to do?" Heather cocked her head to one side, looking like a little bird. It was hard to stay mad at anyone who looked that innocent.

"I don't know. I'll think of something."

They traversed the maze of tables back to their booth, just as everyone was figuring out the bill.

"Here," Christy offered, pulling the $50 from her pocket and tossing it on the table. "Uncle Bob's contribution."

"Are you sure?" "Really?"

"Yeah, it's fine. Go ahead."

They decided to leave the waiter a big tip, since the table was such a mess. One of the girls commented that the waiter had seen them pray together before they ate, and it would look pretty bad if they acted spiritual but weren't generous in thanking him for the service.

Christy hung back, waiting for Todd. They walked through the door together as Doug held it open for them. Todd didn't say anything to her, but he didn't walk away when Christy tried to fall into step with him. Tracy came up next to Christy, and Christy noticed that the expression on her face looked a little softer than when they had gone in.

As it turned out, the four of them—Todd, Christy, Doug, and Tracy—walked together down the pier, the girls next to each other in the middle. The wind sliced even deeper now, and Tracy said, "Man, it's cold tonight."

Christy immediately slipped out of Doug's jacket and said, "Here, Tracy. I warmed up a lot in there. Why don't you wear this now?" She meant it as a kind gesture to a good friend, but as Tracy slipped the jacket on, she gave Christy a strange look as if Christy were intruding. Intruding into what? If Tracy was cold, then she wanted a jacket, right? Or else she wanted Doug to put his arm around her, which he hadn't done. Suddenly, the pieces of the puzzle all tumbled together, and Christy saw the whole picture.

Why hadn't I seen this before? she thought. Tracy likes Doug! He was the mystery boyfriend! And here Christy had been interfering all day. That's why Doug asked for more cookies. Tracy had gone to Doug's house yesterday with Todd and given him her box of cookies. No wonder Tracy was all upset at her for skating with Doug and wearing his jacket! *I can't believe I didn't figure this out sooner! What a relief to at least know what the problem is. Now, how am I going to patch everything up?*

Todd didn't say a word on the way home. He dropped Christy off first, which disappointed her.

Before getting out, Christy touched his arm and said softly so the others wouldn't hear, "Todd, could we talk sometime?"

He turned and looked at her, the hurt puppy sag still pulling at the corners of his eyes. In an annoyingly noncommittal tone, he said, "Sure. Whenever."

Doug popped his head between them and said, "Do you want to do something tomorrow, Christy?"

She cringed. Turning her head slightly, Christy could see Tracy looking anything but pleased.

"I promised my aunt I'd spend some time with her tomorrow," Christy answered quickly.

"I know, you guys," Heather piped up. "Let's plan a New Year's party at my house. My mom won't mind. She'd rather have me home than out on New Year's. You want to? I mean we can do something tomorrow, too, if you want to. But we should all get together for New Year's, don't you think?"

Everyone voiced approval and started throwing out suggestions. Christy searched Todd's expression for some indication of when she would see him again. He looked straight ahead and popped Gus into first gear.

"Later," was all he said.

Christy hopped out and slammed the passenger door so hard that she immediately felt as though she should apologize to poor Gus the Bus, who had done nothing to deserve such treatment.

"Sorry, Gus," she murmured as she stood shivering in the driveway, watching the van chug down the street, driving her all-time friends farther and farther away. "Guess everybody got treated a little unfairly today."

CHAPTER EIGHT

The Quiet Woman

Inside the house, the twinkling white lights on the Christmas tree illuminated the living room. Everyone had gone to bed, leaving Christy alone with her thoughts.

What a disaster of a day! Will Todd call me tomorrow, or should I call him to say I'm sorry? But what did I actually do wrong? I didn't mean to spend so much time with Doug; it just turned out that way. Besides, Todd didn't make any effort to skate with me. Maybe I'm the one who should be feeling wounded, not him.

She meandered up to her room and flopped onto her bed. She noticed a letter on her pillow. It was from Alissa, a girl she had met last summer. Christy had admired Alissa and desired to be like her, until she found out what Alissa was really like and how hard her life had been. They had written to each other several times, but Christy hadn't heard from her for months. If this letter was anything like Alissa's previous letters, it probably wasn't filled with good news.

Christy stretched out, took a deep breath, and began reading:

Dear Christy,
    I lost your address in Escondido, so I hope this gets to you all right. I hope you and your family have a good Christmas. A lot has

been going on in my life lately, and I feel as though you're about the only person I can tell all of this to. Please don't think I'm horrible, but Christy, I'm not innocent like you. I wish I were. The truth is, I'm pregnant.

Christy paused, trying to take in this news. Then she went on to finish the letter, but before she got to the bottom of the second page, tears came, making the words bleary.

I thought about having an abortion a few months ago because it seemed like it would make everything easier, and my problem would disappear. But like they say, "Two wrongs don't make a right." I know you must think I'm a terrible person, and I know I never should have gotten myself into this situation, but I did. A friend of mine had an abortion, and she said she wished she hadn't, because years later she still had nightmares about it. She told me that if she had to do it over again, she would have had the baby and then given it up for adoption, I think that's what I'm going to do—give the baby up for adoption. . . .

Christy wiped away her tears before finishing the letter. She felt so bad for Alissa, but the end of the letter was a little more encouraging.

. . . I have only about three more months to go, so, as you can imagine, I look like a whale.

Remember how in your last letter you said that I should get a Bible and try to find some other Christians? I went to a Crisis Pregnancy Center, and my counselor, Frances, is a Christian. She's helping me and has given me a Bible. I've been going to church with her, too. I knew you would be glad to hear that.

Thanks, too, for saying that you were praying for me. I could use some more prayers, if you think of it. I know it's not going to be easy, but I think I'm doing the right thing.

Well, that pretty much explains why I haven't written for a while. You don't have to write back or anything. I just wanted you to know about the baby, and I hope you'll be praying for me.

Alissa

After reading the letter, all Christy could do was pray. She wasn't sure exactly what to pray, but with tears for Alissa, Christy offered awkward requests to God until she fell asleep.

"Christy dear?" Aunt Marti tapped her long nails on the bedroom door. "Are you up yet?"

Christy barely lifted her head from the pillow. "Yes, Aunt Marti." Her voice came out froggy.

"Good. I thought we could leave in, say, half an hour?"

Christy thumped her head back into the center of the pillow. *Oh, yeah,* she thought. *"Shopping with Aunt Marti Day." How could I have forgotten?*

"I'll be ready," Christy called out, doubting if she could pull herself together in only half an hour, yet determined not to upset her aunt today.

They left the house right on time, according to Aunt Marti's schedule, and Aunt Marti even approved of the jeans and sweater Christy had thrown on. It was the new Christmas sweater Marti had given her.

"Did you have a good time with your friends yesterday?"

"Yes." It wasn't the whole truth, but Christy didn't feel like going into the details with her aunt.

"It's certainly wonderful having Todd back, isn't it?"

"Um-hmm." Christy forced a tight smile. *Come on, Christy, don't say anything negative. Say what she wants to hear and you'll be okay.*

"And that cute little gal Tracy is just a doll, isn't she? Bob said you had a wonderful time making cookies together. I'm so glad you have good friends here, Christina. Dear, dear friends like that are hard to come by, you know.''

Christy didn't say a word—not a word. But her mind was anything but quiet. *My "dear friends" are all ready to kick me out of their lives. It's never going to be the same with them again. Every piece that was left of my friendships from last summer is withered and mangled— just like all those dumb carnation petals I saved in that smelly coffee can. What am I supposed to do with a bunch of dried-up memories?*

Just then Aunt Marti stopped at a red light. The same red light, the same intersection, where last summer, in the middle of the street, Todd had kissed her and given her the bouquet of white carnations. Christy couldn't swallow the wad of self-pity in her throat any longer. Turning her face to the window, she let the tears flow.

It lasted only a moment. The light turned green, Christy faked a coughing spell, and fumbled in her purse for a tissue. With a few quick dabs and clearing of the throat, she had her emotions under control. Aunt Marti hadn't even noticed. What a contrast to last summer, when Christy had gushed her heartaches out all over the place and had willingly let her aunt pick up all the pieces.

Things had changed between them. She no longer appreciated her aunt's dominating personality. Swallowing these emotions was a victory for Christy, and silently she congratulated herself on her maturity and control. Now, if only the incredibly painful knot in her stomach would go away.

"First thing on the schedule," Aunt Marti began, "is your 9:30 appointment at Maurice's. He's going to be amazed to see how quickly your hair has grown!"

"You made an appointment for me to get my hair cut?"

"I knew you wouldn't mind. It's gotten so long, dear, you really are desperately in need of a cut.''

"No way!" Christy popped off. "I am not getting my hair cut!"

Aunt Marti shot a stunned glance at Christy as she maneuvered through the parking lot at Fashion Island Shopping Center. "Christina, I'm surprised at you! What are you saying?"

"I'm saying I do not want to get my hair cut." She said each word slowly and deliberately. "I'm trying to grow my hair out again." She took a deep breath as Marti parked the Mercedes, clicked off the engine, and turned to face her. "You didn't even ask me, Aunt Marti. You could have at least asked me!"

Aunt Marti pulled back like a turtle disappearing into its shell. Her voice came out as controlled as Christy's but softer, more gracious. "I was trying to think of what was best for you, dear."

Silence reigned for a moment. Marti cleared her throat and then literally stuck her neck back out. "Why don't we keep your 9:30 appointment, for a simple wash and blow dry. Then, if you decide to have anything else done, you can tell Maurice exactly how you'd like your hair. Would that be agreeable to you?"

Christy wanted to scream out, "No, that would not be agreeable! Your interference in my life is not at all agreeable!" But she controlled her emotions and answered, "All right." It was no good appearing calm. The searing blob in her stomach grew and grew.

Maurice washed Christy's hair and chatted brightly with Aunt Marti. Christy didn't say a word. After the conditioning and rinsing, he wrapped a towel around her head and directed her to his styling area. Christy looked at herself in the mirror. Her expression was disturbing: hard and cold with clenched teeth. She didn't like it.

The words to a Debbie Stevens song she had heard at Todd's flashed into her mind, and she began to sing them inside her head, like a prayer:

Touch this heart, so full of pain,
Heal it with Your love.
Make it soft and warm again,
Melt me with Your love.
I don't want to push You away;
Come back in,
Come to stay.
Make me tender, just like You,
Melt me with Your love.

Maurice removed the towel and fluffed up her hair with his fingers. "So long!" he exclaimed. "So badly in need of a trim. Next time do not wait so long before you come see me."

Christy met his gaze in the mirror, and she spoke gently but firmly, "I'm letting my hair grow. I don't want it cut today."

"But, perhaps, just a tiny trim, then?" Maurice already had the scissors in his hand.

"No. I want it to grow."

Maurice and Aunt Marti exchanged glances in the mirror behind Christy. She felt awful. She didn't want to be a brat. *Make me tender, just like You, / Melt me with Your love.*

Maurice slapped the scissors down onto the counter and stepped briskly away from the chair. Aunt Marti shot her a look that said, "Oh, now you've done it! You've offended the best-known hairstylist in Newport Beach!"

Christy offered Marti a weak smile—not a mean smile, a nice smile, a soft smile. A smile that showed her heart was melting but not her determination. She knew what she wanted, and no one could change her mind.

Maurice plopped a large book of hairstyles in Christy's lap. He quickly thumbed through the section showing longer styles. "Like this?" he pointed to a picture of wavy, shoulder-length hair parted on the side. Carefully studying the picture, Christy melted a little more. "That's pretty. I like that style. But my hair doesn't have that much body. It just frizzes."

"Aha!" Maurice announced, snatching the large book and snapping it closed. "I shall give you a wave."

"You mean a perm?"

Aunt Marti stepped forward. "Christy, would you like to have a perm put in your hair today, darling?" She said it as though she were talking to a toddler, exaggerating each word, to make sure Christy was in agreement with the idea.

"I hadn't even thought of it, but I guess that would be okay. That way I can keep my hair long."

Aunt Marti spread her lips in a tight smile. "As long as you're sure that's what you want, dear."

Christy felt the emotions gurgling inside her stomach again. "Yes, Aunt Martha. That's what I'd like. As long as it's just wavy like the picture. I don't want it curly."

"Yes, all right then," Aunt Marti said, sitting back down. "Okay. Good." She motioned for Maurice to go to work.

It seemed that everyone was relieved several hours later when Maurice stood back to admire his handiwork. Christy's hair looked good—really good—and she loved it. Even though the wave had drawn her hair up a little shorter, it made it look thick and full all around.

Christy shook hands with Maurice and thanked him, telling him what a great job he had done. He looked pleased. Aunt Marti looked pleased. "Would you like to do some shopping, Christy? Or should we grab a bite to eat?" Marti asked.

"Doesn't matter to me."

As if Christy had just relinquished the reins on a team of snorting horses, Aunt Marti snatched them up and off they thundered, in and out of small specialty shops. Christy found a clip for her hair, nail polish, a collapsible mirror for her purse, and a pair of black shoes on sale. Nothing too exciting, yet Aunt Marti seemed delighted with every choice Christy made. It was clear that anything Christy wanted, she could have.

But Christy didn't go wild, picking out clothes and accessories to her heart's content. She felt spoiled, and she didn't like that. She also felt controlled, and she really didn't like that. Plus she didn't want to be shopping. She wanted to be back at the house, doing whatever she could to clear things up with Todd. And every minute she spent with her aunt seemed to be pulling her farther and farther away from him.

At 2:30, Aunt Marti announced it was time for lunch. Christy suggested they go home and make a salad, but Aunt Marti insisted they drive to Corona del Mar. She parked in front of a tiny restaurant on the Coast Highway called The Quiet Woman. The old English tavern sign hanging over the front door showed a headless woman. Apparently, she was "the quiet woman."

Settling comfortably into their secluded booth, Aunt Marti ordered Veal Oscar for herself and the same for Christy before asking, "Does that sound good to you, Christy?"

"Sure. Doesn't matter." Actually, she would have preferred a hamburger. But it didn't matter, as long as they could have a nice, quick lunch, and she could get home and try to work out some of the complications in her life.

The waiter placed their beverages before them. Christy waited until he left before she quietly bowed her head to pray.

"You've really taken your religion to heart, haven't you, Christy?" Aunt Marti asked.

Christy felt a little embarrassed that her aunt figured out that she had been praying. "Our family always prays before meals," Christy said.

"Yes, I realize that, dear. However, I've noticed you do it even when your parents aren't around. It's something you do for yourself, and that's worthy of a compliment, don't you think?"

Christy shrugged. "I guess so. I never thought of praying as something a person would be complimented on."

Within minutes, the waiter stood before them, delivering the savory dishes and filling their water glasses. Christy cautiously took a bite and decided the Veal Oscar tasted pretty good. Aunt Marti looked extraordinarily delighted with the meal and continued the conversation between tiny bites.

"I'm pleased to see how you're maturing, Christina. I must say, I had some concerns several months ago in Palm Springs when you and your girlfriends snuck out of the hotel room in the middle of the night."

Christy opened her mouth to defend herself, but Aunt Marti calmly waved her fork as a signal to just listen. "There's no need to discuss that night, and I wouldn't have even brought it up, except to say that I'd like to have more input in your life."

Christy waited for her aunt to go on. She felt defensive, anticipating some kind of criticism, which Aunt Marti could dish out like no one else.

"I felt you were reluctant to spend this time with me today. Over the last few days, you've been completely absorbed with your friends, and I can understand that. However, I feel you're making it difficult for me to get involved in your life. I'm proud of the way I see you taking a stand for what you want. But I would like it if you would discuss things with me more and ask my opinion. I truly feel that I can do for you and give to you what no one else can."

Christy squirmed uncomfortably. She loved her aunt, yet she never liked the way Marti tried to mother her.

"I don't know how to make it any clearer than to tell you, Christina, that you are the daughter I never had, and I see you as that—my daughter. I want only the very best for you. Do you think you can understand what I'm saying?"

Christy nodded. She understood perfectly. It was just that she didn't want another mother—or an agent or whatever it was that Aunt Marti saw herself as.

"I see great potential in you, dear. Perhaps more than what your parents see. I could truly make something out of you. You've got the figure, the face, the personality . . . why, you could really be somebody!"

Never before had compliments stung so cruelly. Aunt Marti charged on, apparently not reading the pain in Christy's face.

"I see you becoming the kind of young woman who stands out in a crowd. If you will only allow me to be more involved in your life, I can teach you how to become someone who can get anything she wants—a stunning young woman who makes a lasting impression. Someone like, well, like your friend from this summer. You know, Alissa."

Twang! Everything inside Christy snapped.

"Like Alissa? That's what you want? You want me to become like Alissa?"

"Lower your voice, dear."

"Ha!" Christy laughed aloud, then lowered her voice just a pinch. "It just so happens, Aunt Martha, that Alissa is pregnant!"

Aunt Marti's mouth dropped open, her eyes doubled in size.

"The baby will be born before she even graduates from high school. Is that what you want for me, too?" By now the tears streamed down Christy's face. She didn't care who saw her or what they thought of her.

Not so with Aunt Marti. She rose swiftly, as if something were chasing her. Quickly fumbling with the check, she tossed it back on the table with a couple of $20 bills.

Christy wiped her eyes and followed her spooked aunt as she

blazed a trail through the center of the restaurant and scurried to the car.

Now I've blown it! Why didn't I keep my mouth shut? Christy felt miserable.

Aunt Marti slammed the door and thrust the car forward into the flow of traffic. However, the traffic was clogged on the Coast Highway, causing them to travel a few feet, jerk to a stop, travel a few more feet, then come to another quick stop, with Aunt Marti's foot hard on the brake. At this rate, it could take half an hour to get home.

Christy spoke up, anxious to smooth things over. "Can you see why I don't want to be like Alissa?"

Aunt Marti nodded, without looking at Christy, then slammed on the brakes again.

"I just want to be myself," Christy said softly. "No, actually, it's more than that. I want to be the person God wants me to be."

"That's fine, Christina. Very noble. However. . . ."—Marti paused and pressed extra hard on the brakes so the car lurched, as if for added emphasis—". . . life doesn't always go the way you think it will or the way you want it to."

A heaviness hung between them. Christy knew Aunt Marti didn't understand. But then maybe Christy didn't understand completely either.

The car jerked to another stop, and Marti started coughing. It was a fake, choking kind of cough. Christy thought she saw tears in her aunt's eyes.

What's wrong with me? Christy thought. *Why am I making everybody I know get mad at me? I can't do anything right!*

"Aunt Marti?" Christy felt emptied of all her determination. "I'm sorry. I didn't mean to upset you."

Marti didn't respond.

They drove the rest of the way home in agonizing silence.

When they pulled into the driveway, a yellow Toyota four-wheel-drive truck followed them and parked in front of the house. It was Doug's truck. David sat in the front seat beside him, all smiles.

"We had more fun than you did," David sang out. He bounded from the truck and met stone-faced Christy and Marti in the driveway. "We went skateboarding."

"David," Aunt Marti exclaimed, "you've ruined your brand-new jeans!" Angry words tumbled from her mouth. Christy knew that poor David was receiving verbal blows that were meant for her.

"I know, I kind of wiped out a couple of times," David said sheepishly, all the adventure draining from his voice.

"Go inside and change immediately!"

Without a word, David ran into the house. Christy felt awful for him.

Doug had slowly made his way to where Christy and Aunt Marti were standing, hanging back until the conflict passed. Marti turned to Doug and smiled; she was poised and charming and glossy.

Christy cleared her throat, harnessed her emotions, and quickly made the introductions, explaining that Doug was a friend of Todd's. Doug then said that he knew Christy had gone shopping today, but he thought he would swing by anyway. Since Christy wasn't back yet, he had taken David skateboarding.

Marti looked pleased and said, "How gracious of you, Doug. It's wonderful to meet you. Christy, why don't you invite your friend to stay for dinner, if he'd like? I'm not sure what's planned, but"—she turned to Doug, gushing with sweetness—"you're welcome to join us."

"Thanks," Doug said, without committing himself.

Aunt Marti excused herself, and Christy and Doug stood in the driveway.

"Your hair looks nice," Doug said. "Did you have it fixed today or something?"

"I got a perm. I'm letting it grow," she said with a certain determined look in her eyes.

Doug half smiled and said, "Oh, yeah. You look good in long hair." Then he sniffed. "It smells like flowers or something."

"It's this conditioner stuff they put on my hair," Christy explained. She scooped up the end of her hair and pulled it toward her nose. "I think it smells like green apples."

"Is that what it is?" Doug said. Then, in a natural gesture, he put a hand on her shoulder and leaned over, nuzzling his nose into her hair right above her ear.

At that very second, Christy heard an all too familiar sound. She looked out at the street and caught a glimpse of Gus the Bus chugging past the house. *Oh no! What should I do?* she thought frantically. She couldn't see Todd's face, but she knew he had seen Doug leaning over her, smelling her hair. Todd sped on down the street, as if he hadn't meant to stop at all.

"You're right," Doug said, pulling back, completely unaware of what had just happened. "It does smell like green apples."

Christy felt like yelling at him, but she stood in her frozen position and just stared past him at the back end of Gus, turning at the corner. *I can't believe that just happened!*

"I stopped by so I could talk to you, if that's okay," Doug said.

"About what?" Christy snapped.

Doug pulled back a little and then said, "Well, could we sit inside my truck a minute?"

"Okay, I guess so." Christy calmed herself down.

Once inside the cab of the Toyota, Christy's eyes kept darting up and down the street, just in case Todd returned. She wished he would, but then she wished he wouldn't, because everything felt so mixed up right now. She needed to deal with one thing at a time. Doug first.

"Well, I hope this doesn't come across the wrong way or anything. I'm not sure how to say it."

For the first time, Christy focused on Doug. He looked serious. "Go ahead, Doug. You can tell me."

When he hesitated, she added, "I think you know you can trust me." Even as she heard the words come out of her mouth, Christy wasn't sure she knew what she was getting herself into.

"I know I can trust you," Doug said. "I noticed that when I first met you. You're very approachable. You make people feel as though they can come and talk to you about anything."

Oh sure! Real approachable, Christy thought. *Is that why everyone I know is furious with me at the moment?*

Then Christy remembered Alissa's letter. Alissa had poured out her heart, yet Christy barely knew her. Alissa had said, "I feel like you're about the only person I can tell all this to."

Doug jumped right in. "What I wanted to say is that, well, I'll just say it. I'm taking Tracy out tonight."

"You are?" Christy said excitedly. She impulsively leaned forward and grabbed him by the shoulders. "That's wonderful!"

Doug looked surprised and pulled back. Christy quickly let go. She didn't want Todd to drive by again, and this time see *her* holding on to Doug in his truck.

"I wanted to tell you because, well, I care about you, and I didn't want it to hurt our friendship or anything."

"Don't worry. It won't hurt it at all. I'm glad you two are going out."

Doug still looked uncomfortable. "I guess I thought maybe after we went ice-skating and everything that, well, maybe something was starting between you and me, but I wasn't sure. I mean, I know how much you mean to Todd, and I'd never want to come between you two, but still, I feel as though you and I are starting to become good friends, too, and I'd like that to keep growing." He had said everything in one breath and now drew in another breath of courage.

"So, what I want to say is that I want to get to be really good friends with you, and sometimes, if you go out with somebody, then everybody thinks you don't want to be friends with anybody else anymore and that you just want to spend time with that one person, since you're going out with them. You know what I mean?"

He looked so sincere. Christy smiled for the first time in hours. She reached over and squeezed his hand. "Doug, I understand. Really. We can still be friends—really good friends—and just because you're dating Tracy, that won't change anything with us. It might even make it easier."

"What do you mean?"

Christy hesitated. "All I'll say is that I'm really, really, really glad you and Tracy are going out."

"Good," Doug said with a smile.

"Can I ask you one thing?" Christy said. "Does Todd know you and Tracy are going out tonight?"

"No. I haven't talked to him all day."

"Could you do me a favor and let him know?"

"Sure. Why?"

"Just so that he'll know. Okay?"

"Okay." Doug reached over and touched her hair again. "What do they do? Put electrical wires in your hair and hook you up to a generator or something to make your hair puff?"

Christy gave him a look of playful disgust and gently tugged away. "Doug, you need a sister to educate you in the finer areas of life when it comes to women and manners. As a matter of fact, you and Todd both could use a sister."

"You interested in taking the position?"

"Maybe," she answered playfully.

Doug burst out laughing, focusing on the window behind Christy. She turned to see her brother making a grotesque face and drooling on the truck window.

"Then again," Christy said dryly, "it could be I have all the brothers I need at the moment."

CHAPTER NINE

Confiding in Mom

Christy did a lot of thinking that night. Tomorrow her parents were coming back, which meant she needed to clear things up with her aunt. She had only a few more days with her beach friends, and she had to talk to Todd. Plus, she had to make sure everything was okay between her and Tracy. And she wanted to write Alissa right away, but she wasn't sure what to say. The whole muddled mess made her sick to her stomach.

She decided to start with Todd. Slipping on her robe and new fuzzy bunny slippers, she marched to the phone in her aunt and uncle's bedroom. They were downstairs watching TV with David, and she knew she'd have more privacy up here than downstairs. Bravely dialing Todd's number, she coached herself to say whatever came to mind first. All she had to do was get the conversation going and let Todd take it from there.

It rang four, then five times before a deep male voice answered. It wasn't Todd's voice. His dad's maybe?

Christy opened her mouth and . . . nothing came out.

She quickly slammed down the receiver, then stared at the phone as though it were a familiar pet that had just bitten her. It all happened so quickly, and she felt so ridiculous. She didn't dare call him back.

Why did I do that? Why is my heart pounding so fast?

Christy flopped back onto the bed and let out a blurt of nervous laughter, laughing at herself.

So much for brave and daring and getting everything all cleared up with Todd!

Like a meek little mouse, Christy scurried back to her bedroom, her fuzzy slippers leaving tufts of white fluff on the hallway carpet behind her.

She tried calling Todd twice the next morning, but each time she hung up before it even rang.

What is my problem?

Heather called around noon and had all kinds of exciting news about how the party was shaping up for the next night.

"Have you talked to anyone else today about the party?" Christy asked.

"Like who?" Heather seemed to know what Christy was getting at, but Heather also seemed to enjoy making Christy spell it out.

"Well, has Todd said for sure that he's going? I really have to talk to him, Heather."

"Why don't you call him?"

"I tried, but . . ."

"Okay. I'll call him, then I'll call you back and tell you what he says."

"You don't have to, Heather."

"No, I need to call him anyhow, so if I happen to mention that you've been trying to get ahold of him, it won't be a big deal."

Christy sighed into the phone.

"I'll call him right now, okay?"

"I guess." Christy heaved another sigh. "I don't want things to get any more complicated than they already are."

"Don't worry. Everything will work out fine. Look how

wonderful everything is for Doug and Tracy. Tonight he's having dinner over at Tracy's house. Isn't that great? I told her to have her mom invite him."

"That's great!" Deep down Christy meant it, but right now it didn't help to know that Doug and Tracy were together. Their problems might have been solved, but hers weren't. She still hadn't smoothed things over with Tracy, and all this stuff with Heather calling Todd was just part of the games again—games Heather loved to play, but games Christy wasn't so sure she wanted to get caught up in. These games hadn't helped her progress much with Todd in the past.

Why can't I be bold and up front like Doug? He was incredibly caring yesterday when he came over and talked to me privately just to make sure he wouldn't hurt my feelings by going out with Tracy. And Doug is the only one whose personality hasn't changed drastically during the last few days. He acted the same way toward me when he skated with me as he did when he told me he was going to go out with another girl. Now that's an all-time friend. Why can't I be like that?

When Heather called back a few minutes later, she had disturbing news. "Todd said he might not make it to the party. He said he was going to a dinner tomorrow night."

"A dinner? With his dad?"

"He didn't say, but he kind of made it sound like a date or something."

Christy's heart sank.

"I'm sorry, Christy," Heather said.

"That's okay. I just didn't know he was dating anyone."

"He's not, as far as I know. Maybe somebody set him up— you know, an out-of-town cousin of his dad's boss here for the holidays."

"Great."

"But I told him you were trying to get ahold of him. He said his dad just got back from Switzerland, so he's been hanging around the house, spending time with his dad. Maybe you should try calling him again."

"Why doesn't he try calling me, huh? Would that be too much to ask?"

"Don't get so defensive! I tried, okay?"

"I'm sorry, Heather. I know you tried. Thanks. It's just that I thought he was going to be at your party and that would be the perfect time for me to talk to him."

"Well, he said he was going to this dinner thing, but after that he might come by. Why don't you call and ask him yourself?"

"I should."

But she didn't. She couldn't—at least not right away. Right now her feelings, worn thin, couldn't handle another blow if Todd didn't respond the way she needed him to. She knew she should call him.

But she put it off and retreated to the family room, avoiding contact with Aunt Marti and everyone else in the world by tuning into the TV. There, alone, she spent most of the day watching old movies and eating anything she could find—anything, that is, except international cheese.

Christy's parents arrived in the late afternoon, right during the last five minutes of *Captain January*, a Shirley Temple movie Christy had never seen before.

"Christy!" her dad called out as they came into the house. "Please come here and help carry in these bags."

"Okay! In a minute," she called back, her attention glued to the TV.

Dad stood in the doorway of the den and said, "I really need your help now, Christy."

"Okay. I'm coming." Christy jumped up and hurried out to

the car. She knew that tone in her dad's voice and didn't want to get him upset.

"Where should I put it, Dad?" Christy asked when she walked back into the house.

"Downstairs guest room," he answered on his way to the kitchen.

Christy hurried, hoping to catch the final minutes of *Captain January.* She pushed open the bedroom door with her shoulder and stopped. There on the bed lay her mother with her foot in a cast.

"Mom, what happened?"

"It's really nothing. I slipped and fell yesterday. A hairline fracture. Doesn't even hurt, but the doctor wanted me to stay off it."

"Mom, I didn't know."

"It wasn't worth calling to tell everyone. It's not that bad." Mom pushed back her graying brown hair and smiled. "Your dad would probably have me in the hospital by now if the doctor hadn't convinced him I was all right." She propped a pillow behind her back and said, "Thanks for bringing in my bag. So, tell me, did you have a good week?"

Then, as if Christy were four years old again, she climbed onto the bed, buried her head in her mom's shoulder, and cried her eyes out.

The tears lasted only a few minutes. Christy pulled up her head, wiped her eyes, and feeling ridiculous, apologized over and over. *How could I have fallen apart so suddenly?* she thought.

Her mom smiled and handed her a tissue. It had been a long time since they had shared a transparent moment like this. Mom said softly, "Must have been a pretty bad week."

Christy hesitated. "I guess it wasn't all that bad. It's just that everyone is mad at me. And then I came in here, and you're in a cast and I didn't even know." She looked away. "Oh, Mom! My whole life is falling apart."

"You want to tell me about it?"

Christy usually didn't tell her mom many of the details about what was going on with her friendships, but now that all the doors were opened between them, she decided to go for it.

In one long sentence, Christy explained all about Todd and about Tracy's being jealous of her, and about Doug and how that had worked out, sort of; but she still hadn't seen Tracy, and Heather was having a party tomorrow night, but Todd might not come.

"What time is this party?" Mom asked. "And where is it?"

Christy told her and then asked, "I can go, can't I? I have to talk to Todd—I mean, if he comes. But I mostly need to talk to Tracy and make sure she understands I wasn't trying to get Doug away from her."

"I suppose you can go. It sounds as though everything will work itself out, once you see your friends and have a chance to talk."

Christy nibbled nervously on her fingernail.

"You don't look too convinced of that," her mom said. "By the way, your hair looks very nice. Did Marti take you to have it done?"

Christy nodded. "Except we kind of got in an argument at lunch, and we're still both sort of avoiding each other."

"What happened?"

Christy never thought it could be this easy to talk with her mom. Probably because an opportunity like this had never come up. Or maybe because she never tried, because she had assumed her mom wouldn't understand. But what had Uncle Bob said on Christmas morning? Something about her parents being young once. And her mom grew up with Marti. Of course she would understand how hard it was to communicate with her sometimes.

Christy told her about Maurice's and how Aunt Marti had told her at lunch that she was the daughter she had never had. Mom's usually clear blue-gray eyes clouded.

"What else did Marti tell you?" she said.

"That she wished I were like Alissa, a girl I met here this summer."

"Yes," her mom said thoughtfully, "I remember Marti's mentioning her before."

"Mom," Christy said, looking her in the eyes, "I got a letter from Alissa a few days ago, and she told me a whole bunch of stuff." Christy paused and then plunged in. "Mom, Alissa is pregnant."

Mom looked serious in a soft, understanding way.

"When she found out," Christy continued, "she went to a counseling center. See, in the last letter I wrote her, I told her I was praying for her and that maybe she could find some other Christians. So she called around until she found this pregnancy center that is run by Christians, and they've been helping her."

Mom listened intently.

"She also said that her counselor at the pregnancy center, a lady named Frances, was taking her to church. That was about the only good news in the whole letter."

"Where does Alissa live?"

"In Boston, with her grandmother. Her dad's dead, and her mom is in an alcoholic rehabilitation center."

"Oh, my," Mom sympathized, shaking her head. "Did you tell Marti all this?"

"No." Christy hung her head. "When Aunt Marti told me she wanted to make me into somebody like Alissa, I blurted out the part about her being pregnant."

"What was Marti's reaction?"

"She wouldn't talk to me. I apologized, but she's barely talked to me since."

Mom leaned forward on the bed, stuffed a pillow under her cast, and then sat up as straight as possible. "Christy, there's something you should know."

Now it was Mom's turn to be open and honest, and Christy wasn't sure what to expect.

"Marti had a daughter once." Mom's words came out painfully soft. "A week before you were born, Marti gave birth to a baby girl."

Christy stared at her mom in disbelief.

"The baby was three months premature and was born severely brain damaged. The doctors did what they could, but the baby died." Mom paused, then added, "Christy, you were born the next morning."

Christy let the tears flow. "I never knew. Mom, how come you never told me?"

"It isn't something Marti ever talks about—with anyone."

"Why didn't they have another baby?"

"They tried. Even though the doctor advised against it, they tried. Marti wasn't able to conceive."

"Why?" Christy felt a rush of a whole string of emotions she had never felt before for her aunt.

"Well . . ." Mom chose her words carefully. "Sometimes a person makes a decision that seems the easiest or best at the moment, but later they find that choice had a price."

"I don't understand."

Mom paused and said, "If Marti opens this topic up with you sometime, then you ask her about it, all right?"

Christy remained quiet, remembering a collage of conversations, arguments, and actions of her aunt that hadn't made sense until this moment. No wonder Marti said Christy was the daughter she never had. She was more like the replacement for the daughter Marti had and then lost.

"Mom? Did they name her, the baby?"

A gentle, endearing expression swept across her mom's face. "Johanna. Johanna Grace. She was named after our grandmother, your great-grandmother."

"Johanna," Christy repeated. "That's pretty."

Mom nodded. "It was almost your middle name. Your father and I planned to name you Christina Johanna. But after little Johanna passed away, well . . ."

Christy blotted the last few runaway tears and then shook her head. "This is kind of freaky, Mom. I mean, finding out I almost had a different middle name and that I had a cousin I never knew about. Are there any other big family secrets I should know?"

Mom thought a minute. "I think those are the only ones you need to know at this point. I never would have told you about Johanna, but I felt it would help you understand your aunt better. She truly loves you, Christy. I think you know that. You don't have to go along with everything she has in mind for you, but do understand that she's acting out of a motherly instinct. You mean an awful lot to her."

Just then Dad stepped into the guest room and asked, "Can I get you anything?"

"No, thanks, I'm fine. It feels much better propped up like this." Mom pointed to her pillow-elevated cast.

"Dad," Christy said, turning around on the bed and facing him, "I was wondering if I could go to my friend Heather's house tomorrow night. She's having a New Year's party. Her parents will be there and everything."

Dad sat down on the edge of the bed and shook his head. "I don't like the idea of your being out on New Year's Eve."

"But I'll be completely safe at Heather's house. It's not very far from here. And it's the last chance I'll have to see all my friends."

"Your aunt just told me you spent most of your week with your friends," Dad said.

"Not really. We went ice-skating one day. That was all." Christy was worried. It looked as though her dad wasn't going to let her go to Heather's party and that meant she might not see Todd again.

"Let me give it some thought, Christy. We don't know your friends here, or what their home situations are like."

Christy's heart sank deeper and deeper. *He might really say no, and then what am I going to do?*

"We can talk about this later, Christy," Mom said. "Would you do me a favor and see if Marti needs help getting dinner going?"

"From the looks of it, it's all ready," Dad said.

"All ready? What are we having?" Mom asked.

"Judging by what I saw on the counter, we're having a buffet of international cheeses."

Mom groaned and shook her head.

"Oh, please," Christy said, "anything but that!"

CHAPTER TEN

Wrong Number

Actually, they had chicken for dinner. Or, maybe it would be more accurate to say that Christy was a chicken at dinner. She intended to bring up the subject of Heather's party again, with a sneaky, back-door approach. She thought that if Uncle Bob heard about the invitation, he might talk her dad into letting her go. But she chickened out.

After dinner, the three "boys" went out front to play with David's remote-control car. Christy cleared the table by herself and loaded the dishwasher while her mom and Aunt Marti talked in the living room. Marti had barely looked Christy in the eye since their conflict the day before, and that bothered Christy a lot. She didn't know if she should apologize again or let it rest.

The solitude of the kitchen helped Christy think through some of the heavy thoughts that relentlessly pounded her. It seemed as though every relationship she had was on "hold" right now. Sprinkling the dish soap into the dishwasher, she closed the door and snapped the "On" switch. The machine whirred, and Christy leaned against the counter, wishing she could wash away the uncomfortable events of the past week as easily as the dishwasher cleaned the dishes.

The phone rang. It rang two more times, and Christy answered it.

"Hello?"

"Hey, Christy. How's it going?"

"Todd?"

"Yeah. How's it going?"

Christy leaned against the counter. After all her schemes to talk to him, now she couldn't think of what to say. "It's going okay, I guess."

"You sure?" Todd asked, his voice calm and even.

Christy hesitated. *What should I say? The truth?*

"Actually, things have been better." *There. That was truthful.*

One of those terrible pauses followed—a pause that made Christy feel completely insecure, thinking that Todd must be sitting there on the other end, wishing he'd never called in the first place.

"Tracy said you wanted me to call you," Todd said.

"Tracy?"

"Actually, she said that Heather said that you told her that you wanted me to call you."

Oh, no! Not another one of these triangles!

Christy carried the cordless phone over to the kitchen table and sat down, her free hand supporting her forehead. "Not really, Todd. I mean, I wanted to talk to you. As a matter of fact, I've wanted to talk to you all week. I guess it just hasn't worked out. I didn't tell anyone to relay any message to you, though. At least, not the way it sounds like I did."

Todd didn't say anything.

Christy felt she needed to speak up and tell him how she felt. "Todd? I want you to know that . . ."

Just then Aunt Marti bustled into the kitchen, and Christy instantly silenced her heart and her words.

"Yes?" Todd prodded.

Christy turned away from her aunt, who was retrieving a diet soda from the refrigerator. Calmly getting up from the table and moving over to the window, Christy pretended to be watching her dad maneuver the remote-control car around the driveway. With her voice lowered, she continued. "It's just that this week hasn't exactly gone the way I hoped it would. I thought we'd have more time together."

"I know."

That's all you're going to say, Todd? "I know"? I'm pouring my heart out here, and all you say is "I know"?

Another awkward pause. Then Todd spoke as if he had worked hard and long at choosing the right words.

"This week didn't exactly go the way I thought it would either. But you know what? It's okay. Everything is going to work out. As far as I'm concerned, nothing's changed."

That was all he said. She kept waiting for him to go on, to explain how everything was going to work out. Would he set a time and say that he was coming over so they could work everything out? No, he wasn't saying anything or committing to anything. Aunt Marti slid a glass into the ice cube dispenser in the door of the refrigerator. The ice clanged loudly.

"Sounds as though I'd better let you go," Todd said.

"Oh, no, that's okay." Christy watched her aunt leave the kitchen. "It's all right. What were you going to say?"

"I don't want to keep you from your family or anything."

"It's okay, really, Todd. You're not keeping me from anything."

"We can talk more when I see you. I think I'd better let you go. Later, Christy."

"When?" Christy demanded. "When are we going to talk more?"

But Todd didn't answer. All she got was the dial tone buzzing in her ear. *What do you mean, "Later"? Todd! What did you mean, "Nothing's changed"? Todd!*

Christy marched across the kitchen floor, returned the phone to its cradle, and then bustled into the dining room. There she suddenly came face-to-face with her aunt, each of them looking the other in the eye. Neither of them said anything at first.

Then Aunt Marti lowered her head, her glass of soda in her hand, and mumbled, "Excuse me, dear."

Christy couldn't stand the alienation—the icy distance between them. "Wait a minute, Aunt Marti."

Marti turned.

The frustration with Todd filled Christy with boldness, although the words tumbled out without much finesse. "Aunt Marti, Mom told me about Johanna, and I'm really sorry. I never knew."

Marti's expression grew pinched and fierce. "She what!"

Christy stood her ground and tried to soften her approach. "Mom told me about your baby girl and how—"

"She had no right to tell you that!"

"Well, I'm glad she did because it helped me understand why you do so much for me and why you—"

Marti sharply drew up her index finger and wagged it inches from Christy's nose, growling through clenched teeth. "You don't understand a thing, Christina. Not a thing!"

Then she pivoted on her heels and marched off to her bedroom, leaving Christy alone in the dining room. She could hear the back door open and her dad's voice filling the kitchen. Christy fled upstairs to her room, shattered to the core and determined to stay away from everyone.

Wasn't talking supposed to clear up conflicts? Weren't people supposed to get their feelings out in the open? Then, why did it become more of a mess when she talked to her aunt; and why, oh why did she feel more confused and frustrated after talking to Todd?

What am I doing wrong? Christy thought in despair. Throwing herself on the bed and curling up in an angry ball, she let all her thoughts go racing around and around. When they slowed long enough for her to recognize them as more than blurs and flashes, she carefully tried to sort them all out. The quiet helped her calm down.

After a long while, Christy reached for her Bible. She turned to the book of 1 John, since Tracy had suggested they all read it that week. That obviously wasn't going to happen, but Christy thought maybe she should try reading the short book. About halfway through the first chapter, she remembered a verse she had seen in Doug's truck. It was written out on a 3x5 card and attached to his visor. It was something about God knowing our thoughts and she remembered it being in Psalm 130-something.

Christy found Psalm 130 and started reading verse one: " 'Out of the depths I cry to you, O Lord.' "

Boy, that's sure how I feel tonight.

She kept reading chapter after chapter. Some of the verses didn't make any sense at all, and she skipped some parts. But then she came to Psalm 139 and found Doug's verse: "O Lord, you have searched me and you know me. You know when I sit and when I rise; you perceive my thoughts from afar. You discern my going out and my lying down; you are familiar with all my ways. Before a word is on my tongue you know it completely, O Lord."

Closing her Bible, she lay back with her hands behind her head and stared at the ceiling. "Lord, if You already know what I'm thinking and what I'm going to say, then why do You let me blow it all the time? Why can't You control my life a little better?

Every day I have to keep coming back and coming back and telling You how I messed up. Don't You get tired of it? Couldn't I just do things right for once, so I wouldn't have to keep asking You for a second chance? I don't want all this agony with my friends and family. I want everything to work out smoothly. And I want You to be happy with me."

She meant that prayer. She meant it with all her heart. And she knew God had heard her. After all, He knew all her thoughts, didn't He? Then why was everything the same the next morning? Nothing seemed to have changed. Aunt Marti ignored Christy at breakfast. The subject of the party didn't come up on its own, and Dad didn't seem overly approachable, so Christy bit her tongue and waited.

Then, when she had a moment alone with her mom, she told her how she had mentioned Johanna to Aunt Marti the night before and how much it had angered Marti. She was hoping to open the door to a deep, meaningful talk with her mom again.

Mom only groaned and shook her head. "Why, oh why did you say anything, Christy? I didn't tell you so that you could throw it back at Martha."

"I didn't throw it at her. I mean, I wasn't trying to. I wanted her to know that I knew."

"Why?"

"Because it changed everything for me. Now I understand her a lot better, and I know why she treats me the way she does. You said that I could ask her about it."

"No, no, no, no, no. What I said was that if Marti ever opens up the topic that she could tell you the details because I don't feel I have the liberty to do that. For now, we'd be better off dropping the whole subject."

"Okay. I'm sorry. I didn't mean to—"

"I know you didn't," Mom said softly. "Would you mind

handing me that pillow over there?"

She pointed to a throw pillow on the corner chair in the living room. Christy picked it up and handed it to her mom, who stuffed it under her cast.

"Mom?" Christy ventured. "Do you think I'll be able to go to the party at Heather's tonight?"

"I don't think so, Christy. Maybe next year, when you're older."

"But, Mom, I really need to see my friends and talk to them like I told you." Surely her mom would sympathize and see how important this was to Christy. She could talk her dad into it, couldn't she?

"I know it'll be disappointing, Christy. But there will be other New Year's parties. I'd say the best thing you could do would be to call Tracy and Todd and try to work things out over the phone."

What a crushing blow! What had Uncle Bob said about her parents being teenagers once? Well, maybe they were, once. But at this moment, Christy could not believe her mother or father ever had been typical teens. If they had been, they would see the importance of the whole situation.

The more Christy thought about it, the more she realized she had better take her mom's advice or else she'd go back home tomorrow and have missed the opportunity to talk to either of them.

But why did she have to be the one to call them? Why couldn't Todd just call and have a normal conversation? Why did he have to be so confusing?

Christy finally decided that maybe she should go ahead and call Tracy and Todd. It would be better than going back to Escondido with everything completely unresolved. It couldn't hurt.

Slipping upstairs, she drew in a breath of courage and dialed Tracy's number.

"Hello?" It was Tracy's mom.

"Is Tracy there?"

"No, she's out with some friends. Would you like to leave a message?"

"Do you know when she'll be back?"

"This afternoon sometime."

"I guess I'll try calling her then. Thanks. Bye."

Christy hung up and stared at the phone. It was now or never. She had to call Todd. He answered on the first ring, and she bravely said, "Hi, Todd?"

"Yeah?"

"Hi, it's Christy."

"I know."

"Could I talk to you for a minute?"

"Sure."

What is all that noise in the background? "Todd, I was wondering if you were going to Heather's party tonight."

"Maybe."

"Well, I'd really like to have a chance to talk to you. I'm going home tomorrow."

"Okay."

Come on, Todd! Can't you answer in more than one-word sentences? And what is all the commotion in the background? "So, when can we talk?"

He answered with half a laugh, "Later."

Christy lost it. "What do you mean, 'Later'? Is it too much to ask you for a straight answer? What is all this, 'Yeah, okay, maybe'? Why can't you ever commit to anything?"

Todd didn't respond. She had never yelled at him before. She could hear him breathing, and then she clearly heard Doug's voice in the background say, "Come on, Todd! You going to sit on the phone all day?"

So Doug was there. That meant Tracy must be, too. All the "all-time friends" got together at Todd's, except no one thought to invite her. That hurt!

Suddenly, she realized that she had told herself for months that her relationship with Todd was unchanging, but that wasn't true. She didn't know where she stood with him. Ever!

"Hey, Christy—" Todd began, but she cut him off with words she didn't plan on saying and regretted as soon as she let them spill out.

"Oh, excuse me," she said, sounding bitter and cold. "I must have the wrong number. I thought you were somebody else."

She slammed down the receiver and burst into tears. An instant later, the phone rang. She let it ring twice before controlling her shaking voice and answering.

"What's going on?" Todd asked.

She couldn't answer.

"Christy?" His voice softened and cut through to her heart. "I don't know what's going on, but whatever I did to tick you off like this, hey, I'm sorry, all right?"

"It's not your fault, Todd." She blinked and swallowed the tears. "It's just me. Really. I'm sorry I bothered you."

"You didn't 'bother' me." Todd sounded irritated; then he mellowed out and said, "Listen, let's just let it go for now. We'll talk some more later, okay?" It was a statement. One of Todd's "this is how it is" factual statements. It left Christy feeling even more empty.

"Okay," she said hoarsely. Then, flippantly, she used Todd's own word back at him: "Later," and she slammed down the receiver.

So just when are we going to talk, Todd? You have all your friends over today, and tonight you have some big date. And even if, by some miracle, my parents let me go to Heather's party, would we even be able to talk then? Or are you going to bring your date with you—if you even show up, that is!

Suddenly, David burst into the bedroom. "Christy? Oh there you are. You want to go out and play volleyball on the beach?"

"No."

"You want to ride bikes?"

"No!"

"Come on! Let's go out on the beach."

"I don't want to, David. Just leave me alone, okay?"

"I bet you'd go out if Todd were there!"

Christy sprang to her feet and shoved David out of her way. "Don't ever say that name to me again!"

She stormed from the room as David chanted after her, "Toddy, Toddy, Toddy, Toddy-Woddy, Toddy!"

CHAPTER ELEVEN

The Mandolin Player

"Christy?" Uncle Bob's voice was extra gentle through her closed door. "I wanted to let you know we're having some company for dinner tonight. It's sort of a tradition. We have a formal dinner every New Year's Eve. You'll need to dress up."

She didn't want to dress up. She didn't want to eat dinner. And she certainly didn't want to go to Heather's party. She was convinced that she had no true friends in Newport Beach. She would be better off going home, although things weren't much better there, were they? Every time she was around people, she made them and herself miserable. Why couldn't her life be nice and calm and simple and uncomplicated?

A few minutes later, her dad's thick hand pounded on the door. "Christy?"

She sat up straight and cleared her throat. "Yes?"

Dad opened the door and came over and sat next to her on the bed. "About this party at your girlfriend's house tonight. I've given it some thought and talked it over with your mother. We've decided that you can go."

"Well, I don't really want to go now," Christy said in a mousy voice.

Her dad looked at her in disbelief, then shook his head. "You might change your mind later. Just make sure you put your best dress on and join us for dinner at 6:00, all right?"

Christy nodded. She made no attempt to go enjoy her last day of Christmas vacation. Instead she stayed in her room, struggling with herself, her dreamlike approach to life, her anger and frustration, and the way she felt she was always failing God, no matter how hard she tried.

This week had turned out to be a great disappointment. Her Christian friends had let her down, Todd had left her completely disillusioned, and the whole thing with Alissa's and Marti's secrets left her weak and empty. That's how she felt. Empty. Completely empty.

At 5:15, she glanced at the clock and decided the battle needed to come to an end. Honestly, openly, she prayed, "You know what I'm thinking, don't You, God? You know everything I'm feeling. So why does it have to be like this? I hate falling flat on my face all the time."

A picture came to Christy's mind, something she had seen while shopping the other day with Aunt Marti. A darling little girl in pink tennies was shopping with her mommy. She had blond hair and pudgy cheeks and was just learning to walk. The mother put the toddler down while she looked through a rack of clothes. The toddler took about five wobbly steps before falling down, nose first. The mom scooped up her little angel, who was wailing loud enough for all to hear, kissed her on the nose, then put her back down.

Christy thought the little girl would have stayed seated where the mom put her. But no, she stopped crying, stood up, and took six or seven more awkward steps until she touched her mommy. There she stood, smiling and holding on to her mother's leg.

Now Christy saw herself as that little girl, trying so hard to walk, yet falling every time. "Time for me to get up and try again, isn't it, God?"

Feeling renewed enough to face the family, she sprang into action and showered and dressed in record time. The only really nice dress she had with her was a black one Aunt Marti had bought for her in Palm Springs last fall. It was definitely a party dress, even if the only party she would be going to was downstairs with a bunch of "old raisin" friends of Bob and Marti's.

The dress made her look older than 15—all her friends said so. Her dad, who was always telling her to "slow down," didn't approve of dresses that made her look older than she was—like the blue one Aunt Marti had bought her last summer. Christy had worn it a few months ago to church and then out to lunch with Rick and some of his friends, and her dad had not been happy. Well, the black one was the only nice dress she had with her, and her father had said, "Put on your best dress."

At 6:00, David knocked on her bedroom door. "I'm supposed to come get you," he said.

Christy swung the door open, and the first thing, the only thing, she saw was David's blinking bow tie. "David, you can't wear that!"

"Why not? I'll turn it off. Nobody will even know it blinks. Look, I even wore this dumb pink shirt." He opened his jacket to give the full view of the shirt, but all Christy noticed were the tie wires.

"Come here," Christy said, shaking her head. "If you're going to be rigged, at least hide your wires."

In a few minutes, she had David completely rewired. As she tucked his collar down in the back, David squeezed the button in his pocket, causing his tie to blink twice.

Christy smiled. "I'm sorry about earlier, David. I shouldn't have shoved you. You are my favorite hamster, you know."

"Oh yeah?" David said with a smirk on his face. "Well, you're my favorite beetle."

"Beetle?" She scrunched up her nose.

"You look like a beetle—a black beetle. You're all dressed in black with all that dark stuff on your eyes. You look like a beetle."

Christy rushed over to the mirror in the hallway. Maybe he was right about the eye liner. She never could figure out how to put it on without it getting smeared or globby. Why did it always look good on the girls in the magazines? She quickly dabbed it off her eyelids.

"Come on," David said. "I can hear music down there. Real music."

David was right. As they swept down the stairs together, Christy was certain that the song "Greensleeves" came from a real instrument, not the stereo. And it sounded like a mandolin.

Christy and David saw their mom and dad, dressed nicely but not too formally, seated by the Christmas tree; the hundreds of twinkling lights in the dimly lit room played fancifully across Mom's dark sweater. Uncle Bob, dressed in a black tuxedo with a sapphire blue cummerbund, stood by the fire with a glass of eggnog in his hand. The three adults turned when they saw David and Christy approach the entryway, and Aunt Marti stepped around the corner, dazzling in a sapphire blue gown with silver sequins.

"Don't you two look marvelous! Look, Bob, Christy has on the dress I got for her in Palm Springs. Doesn't she look wonderful?"

Christy looked to her dad to see if he approved. He didn't. She could tell. But he smiled and said, "You sure these two are my kids? I don't ever remember my kids looking like that."

Everyone chuckled, and the music kept playing. Christy stepped into the living room, curious to see where the sweet melody was coming from. A musician, dressed in a black tux, sat in the dimly lit corner by the window, his head down, playing a mandolin.

Christy stood by the couch, listening and enjoying the end of the song. When the mandolin player plucked the last chord, he lifted his head. The gaze from his screaming silver-blue eyes shot across the room and sliced Christy right through the heart.

"Todd?" she whispered.

Todd stood and playfully gave a bow, then fixed his gaze back on Christy. She froze.

"Um, Mom, Dad? Have you met Todd?"

"Yes, we did earlier," Mom said.

"Hey, dude!" David greeted Todd and rushed over to give him a high five.

"Surprised?" Aunt Marti asked, sidling up next to Christy; her expression, her hair, and her dress all shimmered.

Christy nodded, fixing her attention back on Todd. He looked incredibly handsome.

"Good," Aunt Marti stated, apparently quite pleased with her prearranged New Year's surprise. Or had Uncle Bob set this up?

A tiny crystal bell sounded from the dining room.

"Ah!" Aunt Marti looked even more pleased with herself. "Dinner is served. Shall we?"

Then, as if this were some royal ball, Marti offered her hand to Bob, and he graciously escorted her to the dining room. Dad hoisted his wife from her chair with about as much grace as a dairyman lifting a lame calf. They both laughed, and David picked up the crutches and held them for his mother.

Without saying anything, Todd stepped forward and offered Christy his arm as he played along with the "escorting to dinner" game. She slipped her arm through his hesitantly.

"You okay?" Todd asked softly.

She nodded. "Todd? About today on the phone, I'm sorry."

"Hey. Don't worry about it."

But she did worry about it. She had completely given up on their relationship. In her imagination, Todd had been practically engaged to some other girl whom he was going to have dinner with tonight. She never guessed that she was the girl or that this was the dinner he was going to. She felt completely humbled.

At the dining room table, Todd pulled out her chair, and Christy seated herself. Then he sat next to her, swishing the white cloth napkin into his lap as if he dined like this every night.

Christy tried very hard to relax. Todd seemed fully himself, quite at home in a tux at a formal dinner. She never would have imagined it. There was so much she didn't know about Todd.

A maid or some kind of caterer brought in bowls of steaming soup: cream of broccoli. Bob and Marti both eased their spoons into their soup, then noticed that no one else followed.

"Ah, yes!" Bob declared, setting down his spoon. "Would you offer thanks for us, Norm?"

Dad stood and prayed for the food and for the coming year, gave thanks for the past year, and prayed one by one for each person around the table. Christy had never heard him pray so eloquently.

Ever since they had moved to Escondido and become involved in their church as a family, a lot of things had seemed to come alive for them.

"Well, Norman, you've certainly become the preacher," Marti exclaimed after he said, "Amen."

Dad sipped his soup. His bushy eyebrows pushed together like two caterpillars in a head-on collision. "Anyone can pray, Martha. And there certainly is plenty to pray about these days."

Marti didn't reply.

" 'Course," Dad continued, "even if you're a little rusty at it, it never hurts to give it another try."

Marti slowly lowered her spoon. She didn't look offended, merely determined to have the last word. "Some of us have given prayer and God a second try and a third. But then we wise up." She lifted her spoon for emphasis. "And give up!"

Oh no! Christy thought. *Not now, you guys! Don't get into an argument over spiritual stuff now. Not in front of Todd!*

Christy had seen standoffs like this between her parents and aunt and uncle before. She had had her own conflicts with them whenever she talked about her commitment to the Lord. But tonight, Todd changed everything.

"That's what I like about God," Todd said in his matter-of-fact way, crushing a cracker into his soup. "We might give up on God, but He never gives up on us."

"I'm not so sure about that," Bob said.

"You remember King David?" Todd asked. "In the Bible? He was called 'a man after God's own heart.' But he blew it big time: adultery, murder. Still, God didn't give up on him."

No one said anything. They kept eating, politely listening.

"And Moses," Todd continued. "Remember him? Great leader, right? Well, he killed an Egyptian. Then there's Abraham. He lied—said his wife was his sister so that some king would spare him and take his wife instead."

"What a jerk!" Christy interjected.

"Yeah? Well, Abraham did the same thing twice. Still, he's called 'the friend of God.' "

"So, what you're saying," Bob summed up, "is that the people in the Bible were all sinners, not saints. They weren't really heroes. Only imperfect people like the rest of us."

"I don't think that's what he meant," Mom said.

"No, that's exactly what I meant," Todd said. "Like Peter. The guy spent three years living with Jesus, and then the night of

Christ's trial, Peter wimps out in front of a girl and says he doesn't even know the Lord. But Christ didn't give up on him."

"I certainly didn't intend for us to have a religious discussion over dinner," Marti said, lifting a bell and ringing it.

The maid appeared and cleared the soup bowls.

"Spinach salad with hot bacon dressing," Marti announced as the salad was served.

"So you believe, Todd, that God doesn't give up on people; rather, people give up on God?" Bob asked.

Christy couldn't tell if her uncle was agreeing with Todd or trying to trap him.

Todd nodded. "Of course, it's all in the surrender. Our surrender to God. Because even though we blow it, God will forgive us. But only if we surrender and ask Him for that forgiveness."

"Except you have to be sorry," David piped up. "They told us that in Sunday school. You have to be sorry for what you did, not just sorry that you got caught." He pushed up his glasses and put a whole cracker into his mouth.

Mom and Dad exchanged looks of amazement at their little David. Christy couldn't believe they were all talking about God, and no one was stopping them or arguing.

Bob said, "Do you think, Todd, that these people you listed from the Bible deserved a second chance, or should they have been punished for what they did—the murders and everything?"

"They deserved to die. We all deserve to die."

"But God gave them a second chance?" Bob questioned.

"And a third, and fourth, and so on. See, even after a person becomes a Christian, he still blows it," Todd said.

"Then what's the point?" Marti asked, looking irritated yet sounding sweet. "If people are no better off 'saved' or 'unsaved' because they're all 'sinners,' as you say, then why do you 'born-again' people—and I don't mean that offensively, really—but why do you insist that people aren't Christians unless they've been, well, 'born again'?"

Mom and Dad exchanged glances of uncertainty, Bob looked at Todd, and Christy thought, *You know, Aunt Marti, that's a pretty good question. This week it sure doesn't seem to matter if my friends are Christians or not—especially Tracy. Everything got messed up even though we're all Christians.*

Todd leaned back in his chair, and Christy knew he was about to give one of his famous examples. She loved listening to him talk at times like this, and she loved his illustrations.

"It's like a baby. When a baby tries to walk, he falls down."

Christy immediately thought of the toddler she had seen while shopping with Marti.

"Babies don't give up just because they fall. They keep trying until they get better at it. But see, a baby wouldn't even try to walk if he were never born."

Christy thought she saw Marti's face flinch slightly, but she kept listening.

"That's like becoming a Christian. At first you still fall a lot because you're just learning to walk with the Lord. The more you grow, the better you get at it. But you have to be 'born again,' because the spirit side of your life can't grow if it's never been born."

Christy put down her fork and stared at her plate, seeing only a blur of colors. *That's it! That's why I've been falling all the time. I'm just learning. I'll get better as I grow more. It's okay. God understands, and He's right there to pick me up every time I tell Him I'm sorry.* She felt like jumping up and dancing around the table, saying, "I'm not a failure! God gives me second chances!"

"So, Todd, my boy," Bob challenged, "the next question is, when do you believe a person runs out of second chances with God?"

"You don't." Todd looked at Marti. "You only run out of time."

Marti gave Todd a puzzled look as he concluded, "If you die without ever surrendering your heart to the Lord, then the Bible says you'll be separated from Him forever."

Todd got the same tight, watery-eyed expression Christy had seen on his face at Shawn's funeral last summer. He looked down and said deliberately, "There are no second chances in hell."

Marti choked on a spinach leaf, and Bob looked disappointed, as if he figured he and Todd could carry on this theological discussion with no conclusions being drawn and no feathers being ruffled. Not so. From the moments of silent munching that followed, it seemed apparent that Todd had given them all something to think about.

"This salad is delicious," Mom said cheerfully. "Did you say it's hot bacon dressing? It's so good."

Marti slowly pulled back into her take-charge mode, and by the time they cut into their stuffed Cornish game hens, she led the conversation.

"How long have you played the mandolin, Todd?"

"Couple of years. I've played guitar since I was six or seven."

"And where did you take lessons?"

"My dad taught me."

"And what does your dad do?" Bob asked.

"International sales for a computer company in Irvine."

"I thought you told me once that he was a hippie," Christy said, and Todd laughed.

"He was, but then he discovered money."

Here was a whole area of Todd's life Christy knew nothing about. There was so much more she wanted to learn about him. She started to relax and feel a little less guilty about how she had talked to him on the phone earlier. Yet the nagging questions remained: *Where do I stand with Todd? Exactly where is our relationship going? Did he come tonight out of courtesy to Marti, or did he really want to be with me?*

CHAPTER TWELVE

A Time to Talk

"That was delicious," Mom praised her sister as they all rose from the table.

"Shall we have coffee in the living room?" Marti suggested.

They entered the living room and found the manger scene had been moved to the side of the coffee table. In the center sat a silver tray with a silver coffee pot, sugar and creamer, and china cups and saucers. A tray of candies and little round cookies covered with powdered sugar sat next to the coffee service.

"Can I have some candy?" David asked.

"Help yourself," Bob said.

David stuffed a whole piece of chocolate into his mouth, and for the first time during the evening, he squeezed his hidden button. The tie flashed on and off, drawing everyone's attention.

"Yum, yum!" David said, blinking the tie, and enjoying all the attention as they laughed at him.

Marti poured coffee, Christy nibbled on a powdered sugar cookie, and Todd played another song for them. When he finished, Dad said, "Isn't it time you got going?"

Christy looked at Todd. He smiled and shook Dad's hand.

"Thank you, sir. What time would you like Christy home?"

"Twelve-thirty."

We're going to Heather's party? I can't believe this! Christy thought. *My parents are letting me go with Todd!*

"Are you going to the party now? Can I go? Please? Can I go, too?" David whined.

"No, sir," Dad said.

"Aw, why not?"

"This is Christy's night, son. Your chance will come soon enough."

Slipping into the hallway, Christy smiled and thought, *God, You knew about this all along, didn't You? Why was I so paranoid about everything?*

Marti followed her. "Christy, I wondered if you would like to borrow some earrings for your special night."

"Sure," Christy answered, eager to do whatever she could to mend her relationship with her aunt.

"Here." Marti held out a blue velvet box and said, "These are very special earrings. Your uncle gave them to me on our 10th anniversary. We celebrated in Paris that year, and he gave them to me in a little sidewalk café on the Champs-Elysées."

"Paris? Really?" Christy opened the box and exclaimed, "Oh, they're beautiful!" Lifting the exquisite diamond-and-pearl-cluster earrings, she said, "Are you sure it's okay for me to wear these?"

"Of course, Christy. Now don't spoil my fun by saying you won't wear them. It's my way of contributing something special to your memorable evening."

"Thanks, Aunt Marti. I really appreciate it."

The two exchanged warm smiles.

Then, as Marti helped Christy fasten the earrings, she spoke softly. "This was a difficult week for me, Christina. You have a way of getting to the core of a person; did you know that?"

Christy shook her head.

"Hold still," Marti cautioned.

"I wanted to apologize for all the things I said that upset you," Christy said. "I don't know when to be quiet. Maybe I should be more like the quiet woman on the sign at that restaurant."

"No, dear," Marti said. "You keep being yourself. You have tenacity, Christy, and I don't want you to ever lose that."

"I'm not sure I know what that is, but I hope it's good."

Marti brushed a spot of powdered sugar from Christy's cheek, "Yes, it's good." Then, focusing on the earrings more than she needed to, Marti said, "Tenacious women are good at giving second chances."

Christy desperately wanted to say something deep and tender, like in the movies, but all that came to mind was, "Well, then you must be a tenacious woman, too. Maybe that's where I get it from."

"Possibly."

"Ready?" Todd asked, stepping toward them.

"Yes," Christy said, giving Marti a quick hug. "Thanks for being like a second mom to me, Aunt Marti. I really appreciate you. And thanks for letting me wear your earrings."

"You two get going now," Marti said, snapping out of the tender moment. "I'm certain it goes without saying, but Todd, if you have too much to drink, don't try to drive home. We'll be up, so you call us, okay?"

Todd began to laugh, but then he saw that Marti was serious. "Don't worry. I don't drink. Honest."

"Well, it is New Year's, and you don't know what Heather might have at this party."

"If you knew Heather, you wouldn't even think that," Christy said. Then she realized her aunt must be remembering a party Christy went to last summer where the alcohol and drugs were plentiful. That was an experience Christy never wanted to repeat.

"Don't worry," Todd said. "We'll be fine."

Christy waved to her family in the living room and noticed that David was drowning his sorrows in the remainder of the chocolates, his silly tie blinking off and on.

Sorry, David, but this time you can't take him away, Christy thought. *Finally, Todd and I are going to be together.*

Christy had so much she wanted to talk to Todd about, yet oddly enough, they drove the first few blocks in silence. She wanted to get the conversation going, but now that they were finally alone, she couldn't think of a thing to say. Did he feel strange, too?

Just then Todd stopped at a red light. Christy glanced out the front windshield. It was their intersection! This is where he kissed her last summer. Did he remember? Was he thinking the same thing? She glanced at him cautiously. He was looking straight ahead.

The light turned green, and Todd sped on.

"I wanted to ask you something," Todd said, breaking the stillness.

Good! Finally! He's going to start the conversation!

"I've been thinking a lot about Alissa lately. Have you heard from her?"

Alissa! You've been thinking about Alissa? What about us? "Actually," Christy said stiffly, "I got a letter from her the other day."

"How's she doing?"

"Not so well," Christy said, letting down her guard and choosing to give the news to Todd slowly. "She asked me to pray for her. She's going through a rough time right now."

"She needs the Lord," Todd stated.

"I agree," Christy said as they pulled into a tight parking spot at the end of Heather's block. "But she also needs people in her life who can help and support her while she goes through all this."

"Goes through what?" Todd asked, then turned off the engine and faced Christy.

"Todd, she's pregnant."

"How pregnant?"

"What do you mean?"

"How many months along?"

"Five or six. Why?"

"I knew it!" Todd hooted, popping the palm of his hand against the steering wheel. "Man, this is great!"

"Todd!" Christy couldn't believe his reaction. "I just said she's having a baby!"

Todd kept smiling. "You know what, Christy? It's Shawn's baby."

"Shawn's? How do you know?"

"She's five or six months along, right? Well, count backward."

"I don't know. I thought it might be that other guy's—Erik. The one with the black Porsche that she met at Shawn's party."

"Nope, it's Shawn's."

"How do you know that?"

"I know Erik. He never went to bed with her. He tried, but he never did."

Christy thought back to the day Erik had come to Alissa's house and was upset when he found Christy there.

"I wonder if that's why Erik said all those mean things to Alissa the day she left."

"Could be." Todd leaned back in his seat. The glow from the streetlight washed over his face, showing his contented expression.

"Todd, you should see your face right now. I think this whole thing is awful, and you're smiling. I mean, can you imagine how hard it must be for Alissa being pregnant, with no parents around to support her, and she can't even tell the baby's father because he's dead!"

"Don't you see?" Todd said, leaning forward. "She's giving that baby life. Shawn's baby! She could have aborted it. But she chose to give it life!"

"Todd, she got pregnant! That's not such a noble thing. And you're acting as if she's a heroine. From my perspective, she blew it, and now she's suffering the consequences."

"Right. She is. But don't we all blow it sometimes, in one way or another?"

"Well, yes, but—"

"Doesn't God forgive us and give us second chances?"

"I don't know if she's asked God to forgive her."

"True, and that is the first step," Todd agreed. "But she didn't try to solve the problem by having an abortion. She's going to give that little soul a life, and who knows what that kid is going to be when he grows up. He could be the greatest evangelist the world has ever known!"

"What makes you think it's going to be a 'he'?"

"Okay, *she's* going to become the greatest evangelist the world has ever known!" Todd smiled and then looked serious again. "Man, we've got to pray for her and the baby. We need to pray that she'll meet some Christians who will help her out."

"She did meet some." Christy explained about Frances and the Crisis Pregnancy Center. As she did, Todd's expression grew into a full smile.

"Man, this is incredible!"

"Todd, I still don't see why you're so happy about this. I didn't think sin was something Christians were supposed to get all excited about."

Todd laughed at her in a warm kind of way. "I'm not excited about the sin, Christy. You're absolutely right. Shawn and Alissa should never have gone to bed together. That was totally wrong. At the time, I knew about it, and it ate me up inside."

"You knew?"

"Yeah. But the thing is, God's not limited by their mistakes. Don't you see? Shawn and Alissa created a human life. A soul! Even though what they did was wrong, they made something that is going to last forever. A soul!" Todd looked really excited, as though he was about to shout or something. "A soul, Christy! Even angels can't do that!"

Christy's eyes grew wide. Todd amazed her. He absolutely amazed her.

Todd looked at Christy with a new expression: a pleased look. "You do realize, don't you, that Alissa went to that pregnancy center and looked for a Christian because of you. You might have been the one who really saved that baby's life."

Christy shook her head. "I didn't do anything."

"You showed Alissa that you loved her and cared about her. You were a true friend. And that is something." Todd smiled, his dimples showing in the dim light. "Come on," he said. "We'd better get over to the party. Stay there. I'll get your door."

Being with Todd, even though they talked about Alissa the whole time, warmed Christy. She felt as though she had come into a warm house on a cold day. The anger, hurt, and confusion she had felt toward him that afternoon had thawed, melted, and washed away.

When Todd opened the van door and took her hand to help her out, she felt she'd just been given a second chance with Todd. And maybe that was what kept all lasting friendships going—lots of second chances.

Todd kept holding Christy's hand for the half-block walk to Heather's house. It didn't matter to Christy if they ever defined their relationship. She didn't need to know where she stood with

Todd. Not when she had her hand in his, and they were this close.

"Well," Heather exclaimed when she swung open the door, "we were wondering when you two were going to show up. You guys look like you're going to the prom."

Christy felt her cheeks turning red, and Todd looked as though he weren't used to having attention drawn to what he was wearing either.

"Where did you get the tux?" Heather asked.

"My mom. I had to have it for her wedding. She's one of those people who thinks, 'Why rent when you can buy?' "

"Well, you both look like you should be on the cover of some magazine. And Christy, those earrings are unbelievably sparkly. Are they real diamonds?"

"Yes. They're my aunt's."

Heather oohed and aahed while Todd stepped down into the living room and started talking to the guys. Tracy, who had been sitting next to Doug on the couch, came over to Christy.

"Hi," Tracy said. She looked pretty tonight in her pink sweater, with her hair curled full around her heart-shaped face. "Could we go in the kitchen for a minute, Christy?"

"Sure," Christy said, following her to the corner of the kitchen by the window.

"I need to apologize, Christy. I was rude to you that night at Richie's, and I'm sorry."

"It's okay, Tracy. Don't worry about it."

"You sure? No hard feelings?"

"Yes, I'm definitely sure. And you need to know that I honestly wasn't trying to upset you when I skated with Doug. I didn't know you liked him!"

Tracy's face broke into her bright smile. "I know. I didn't tell you, remember?"

"Well, maybe you should have," Christy said with a laugh.

"Then I would have stayed far away from him!"

Tracy reached over and took Christy's arm. "No, I don't ever want you to stay away from Doug or any of these guys just because I like one of them or somebody else likes one of them. I want all of us to be able to hang out together and not play jealousy games. And that's what made me so mad at myself the other day. That's exactly what I ended up doing at the skating rink! Isn't that dumb?"

"No. I know exactly how it can happen. I've been there."

"Well, Christy, if you ever see me doing that again, promise you'll slap me," Tracy said.

They both laughed.

"Only if you promise you'll slap me, too," Christy said, still laughing. "I got caught up in playing games, too, and I'm really sorry, Tracy."

"It's okay. Let's just start over from here."

Just then Doug came up to them. "Christy, you look really nice tonight."

Impulsively, Christy put her arm around Doug's neck, the way he always hugged everybody else, and she gave him a quick hug. Then she quickly turned to Tracy. "That was okay, wasn't it?"

"Of course!" Tracy said. "That's how I want us all to be."

"What was that for?" Doug asked.

"That was for being the most considerate guy I know."

Doug looked at Tracy. "Did I send her flowers without knowing it?"

"No, no, no," Christy said. "When you came over and told me you were taking Tracy out and said that you still wanted to be friends with me, I thought that was the sweetest thing any guy could ever do. You made it possible for me to still feel comfortable around you, even though you and Tracy are together now."

"Wow," Doug said, "that's awesome, Christy."

Heather popped her head around the corner at that moment and said, "Awesome? You still use that word, Doug? Didn't they teach you any new words in college?"

"Hey! *Awesome* is an awesome word!"

"Come on, you guys," Brian called from the living room. "We've got the game all set up."

Tracy and Christy exchanged glances.

"Don't slap me," Tracy teased. "This isn't the kind of game I meant for you to slap me over."

Christy laughed and joined the rest of her all-time friends in the living room.

CHAPTER THIRTEEN

Forever

Christy ended up on the team with Heather, Doug, Tracy, and Brian. Todd was on the opposite team. It was a word-guessing game, in which they drew with felt pens on a big, white easel pad. Within 15 minutes, Todd's team was way ahead.

"These phrases are too hard for my team," Heather whined. "Don't they have any with 'awesome' or 'dude' in them? Doug would guess those a whole lot faster!"

They laughed, and Doug jumped up, grabbed Heather by the shoulders, and shouted, "Come on, you guys, let's throw her in the pool."

Todd and the other guys jumped up and grabbed Heather. She screamed and kicked until they put her back down.

Christy watched Todd, trying hard to remember exactly what it was that afternoon that made her want to scratch him off her list of friends forever. He was everybody's friend, but she was special to him. He had proved that by putting together their breakfast on the beach and by coming to dinner tonight. Why did she need to define their relationship? It was more than "like" and not truly "in love." They were somewhere in-between.

Around 11:00, Heather rounded everyone up and directed them to the backyard, where a fire blazed in an in-ground fire pit a few yards from the swimming pool. Heather handed out marshmallows and coat hangers and had graham crackers and chocolate bars on the picnic table behind them. The gang set to work making S'mores.

Doug started acting silly, bending his coat hanger in half. "Trace," he called, "hand me two marshmallows. Where's Todd? Where did he go?"

Todd called from the picnic table, "Yo, Doug, over here."

Then Doug stood up with the coat hanger across his head and marshmallows attached to either end so they covered his ears. "Todd," he hollered, "check it out! Number 15. Earmuffs."

Todd laughed until the graham cracker in his hand crumbled into dust. As he held his side, tears streamed down his face. Christy had never seen him crack up like that.

"I don't get it," Heather said, looking at Doug and then at Todd.

"It's this stupid book," Tracy explained, shaking her head. "Todd gave it to Doug for Christmas."

"Todd gave one of those books to Doug?" Christy asked.

"Yes, have you seen it? All about what to do with dead hamsters," Tracy said.

"Ewwww!" Heather squealed. "That's gross."

"Yes, I've seen it," Christy replied. She poked her coat hanger into the fire and toasted her marshmallows.

"Todd gave me the same book," Tracy said disgustedly. "Don't you think a guy would have to be pretty strange to give a girl a book like that?"

"Yes, he would," Christy agreed. "Definitely strange." Christy stared into the amber flame and thought about Rick. *Guys give joke gifts like that to their buddies. Rick must see me as a buddy. But then why did he kiss me? You don't kiss your buddies.*

That's when Christy decided that she and Rick were buddies.

They had pushed their relationship into something it wasn't by trying to be romantic. Not that they couldn't end up going out someday. But they definitely weren't at that point now. And it was silly to pretend they were, or to let other people convince them they were. She liked Rick, and she wanted to go back to being buddies—to give their friendship a second chance. To just let it be what it was without trying to make it something it wasn't.

Christy felt as though a weight had been lifted off her shoulders. She knew what she had done was wrong. Even though she wasn't sure how to fix it, she wouldn't give up until she figured it out. After all, she was tenacious, wasn't she?

While Christy was lost in thought, her marshmallows burned, but she didn't mind. She peeled off the burned part and tried again, roasting the sticky white insides. That's how she always toasted them on purpose when she was a kid. She knew how to burn and peel for layer after layer until only the core of the marshmallow was left.

"Look out! Yours are on fire!" Todd said coming up next to her, his eyes still sparkly from the laughter-tears.

Christy pulled her hanger out of the fire and blew. As Todd watched, she peeled the top layer off and popped it into her mouth.

"Trying to give that marshmallow a second chance, I see," Todd teased when he saw her stick it back in the fire.

Christy said, "I think everybody deserves a second chance, even marshmallows."

Just then Doug trotted into the backyard with a big box in his arms. "Look, you guys, sparklers! I've had them since the Fourth of July. Let's see if they still work."

They finished up their sticky S'mores, and all grabbed sparklers and lit them in the fire pit. Suddenly, flashes of glittering light were everywhere. The group laughed and swished sparklers in the air. The fireworks lasted only a few minutes, and then everyone tossed the sparkler sticks into the fire pit. A few people went inside while others roasted one last marshmallow.

Christy joined the group inside and was standing by the kitchen sink, washing her hands, when Todd came up behind her and said, "You about ready to go?"

She gave him a surprised look. "It's not midnight yet. Don't you want to stay?"

"I said I'd have you home by 12:30. I think we should go now."

"Okay," Christy said, still not sure why they were leaving so early. They said good-bye to Heather and the rest of the group.

Todd maneuvered Gus out of the tight parking spot, and Christy said, "Thanks so much for tonight, Todd. For coming to dinner and taking me to the party."

"But you would have liked to have known ahead of time what was going on, right?" Todd asked.

Christy was surprised that he guessed her feelings so accurately. "I like being surprised, but, yes, I guess I got pretty insecure over when I'd see you and when we'd be able to talk."

"That's why we left Heather's early. I wanted to make sure everything was cleared up between us."

"Is it?" Christy asked.

"As far as I'm concerned, it is. Nothing's changed. Is everything okay with you?"

Christy leaned back. "This is probably really stupid to ask, and I'll probably regret it, but, Todd, what hasn't changed? I mean, what are we?"

"What are we?" he repeated, glancing in her direction.

"Are we just friends or more than friends or buddies or what?"

"I don't think there's a word for it. It's something between 'friends' and 'boyfriend-girlfriend,' like you and Tracy were saying the other day at my house."

"So, what does that mean?" Christy hoped she wasn't pushing this too far.

"It means I really care about you, Christy. It also means I don't want to cut you off from any of your other friends."

"Like when we went ice-skating?"

"Exactly. You and Doug were having a great time together. I didn't want to come between you. But to be honest, I felt pretty sorry for myself. I guess I assumed you and I would be together that afternoon."

Christy felt awful when he said that. "Todd, I wanted to be with you that day, too. I guess I also had big expectations of what the day should have been like. Everything got messed up. And then the next day, when you drove by and Doug was smelling my hair—"

Todd laughed. "Is that what he was doing?"

Christy nodded. "I got a perm that day, and my hair smelled like green apples."

Todd laughed again. "Man, when I drove by and saw you two, I felt as though I'd been eating green apples!"

Christy laughed. "Todd, I'm sorry everything got so mixed up."

"I think it was good. It made me think through a bunch of stuff. I ran into your uncle later at the gas station, and he invited me for dinner tonight. Said I'd probably be able to take you to Heather's party if I asked your dad in person, which I did this afternoon. When your dad said it was okay, I was going to ask you because you sounded freaked when you called. But David told me you were in your room and that he wasn't supposed to ever mention my name to you again." Todd grinned, and Christy hung her head.

"I can't believe this! I was in my room all upset over nothing, and the whole time you were downstairs. Can you believe that? I feel so immature right now."

"That's all right. That's kind of how I was that night at Richie's."

They were both quiet for a few minutes; then Christy said, "I guess we still don't know what we are."

"We're friends, Christy. True friends. Real friends. What that means exactly, I guess we'll have to figure out as we go along. One thing I know for sure is that no matter what happens to either of us, no matter what the future holds, we're going to be friends forever."

Christy's voice came out delicate and sincere. "Todd, I feel the same way. No matter where we are between 'like' and 'love,' and no matter where we end up, I want to be your friend forever, too."

At that instant, Todd pulled up at a red light. Without any warning, he stopped Gus, opened his door, hopped out, and ran to Christy's side. Yanking her door open, he grabbed her by the hand and said, "I can't believe it. This is perfect!"

"What?" Christy squawked. "Todd! What are you doing?"

Taking Christy by the hand, Todd tugged her out of the van and led her to the front of Gus the Bus, where the headlights spotlighted them.

"This is it!" he said. "This is where we are. Somewhere in the middle. Kind of like being right in the middle of the street."

Christy's eyes shot past Todd to the stoplight. Then it hit her—this was "their" intersection! They were standing right in the middle of their intersection on New Year's Eve, dressed in their best clothes, and stopping traffic.

"Todd!" Christy laughed. "This is crazy!"

"I know," he said. "Isn't it great?" Then Todd reached inside his tux and pulled out a small, rectangular box wrapped with a white ribbon. Excitedly, like a little boy, he said, "I didn't know when to give this to you, but, hey, now's as good a time as any. Go ahead, open it."

Cars zipped past them, and Christy kept laughing. Only Todd would do this. She tore off the ribbon and paper. Inside the box she found a delicate, gold ID bracelet. "Todd, it's beautiful!"

"Read what it says."

She held it toward the headlights and read the engraved inscription: " 'Forever.' Oh, Todd, this is so perfect. I love it! Thank you so much. It's exactly what we were just saying about being friends forever."

"You noticed that, too?"

The light turned green, and the car behind them honked. Todd stepped around the van and waved them past like a patrolman.

Christy knew the passengers were staring at her, standing there in her fancy black dress, with her aunt's real diamond earrings, clutching the gift box in one hand and the gold bracelet in the other. But she didn't care.

At that very moment Christy knew where she was for perhaps one of the first times in her life. She was right in the middle of the street, right in the middle of her relationship with Todd, and that's right where she wanted to be—nothing more, nothing less. And right now, nothing else mattered.

"Let me help you put it on," Todd said eagerly, stepping back to Christy's side. He slipped the bracelet around her wrist, pinched the tiny clasp open, and tried several times before securing it around her wrist.

Then Todd took Christy's hand in his and said, "I really mean it, Chris. No matter what the future holds, no matter how many other guys you go out with or how many miles separate us, a part of you will always be right here." He patted his chest.

"You're in my heart," he continued. "You're my friend. I

honestly don't know where we go from here, but I'm not worried. God knows. All I know is we're going to spend eternity together with Him. This bracelet is my way of saying, 'Here's my friendship. I promise it to you. It's yours forever.' "

Christy melted. She never imagined Todd had such a romantic side to him. Yet it wasn't all emotions. It was solid and well thought out. The amazing thing was, although she felt incredibly close to Todd at this moment, she also felt incredibly close to God.

Suddenly, a loud boom echoed from a few blocks over, followed by honks and hoots and a screaming cherry bomb sailing through the air.

"Must be midnight," Christy said. "Happy New Year, Todd."

He smiled and wrapped his arms around her. "Happy forever, Christy."

Then he kissed her, twice. First, on the lips, quick and tender, in the middle of the street, in front of Gus's headlights. The second kiss came after hustling her back to her side of the van and opening her door. He kissed her this time on the right side of her forehead, partly in her hair, partly on her eyebrow. It was sweet— a tender, caring, protective kind of kiss.

Todd ran to his side of the van, waving at the car behind them and shouting, "Happy New Year to you, too, buddy!" He popped Gus into gear, and they charged through the intersection, barely making it through before the light turned red.

Christy twisted her wrist back and forth, watching her bracelet catch glimmers of light. "I love this bracelet, Todd."

His jaw stuck out a little more than usual with a proud, satisfied look. "I'm glad you do. Sorry it's late. It was supposed to be your Christmas present, but it took me a while to figure out what to have engraved on it."

"How did you think of 'Forever'?"

"Believe it or not, I got it out of First John. Remember Tracy said she wanted us to read it and talk about what we learned when we got together? Well, even though that never happened, I read it through a couple of times."

"I read it, too," Christy said. "Well, not all of it, but I started it."

"What I got out of it was that God's love for us goes on forever, and that's how He wants us to love each other."

Christy knew Todd was right. She also knew she'd learned a little about being more loving to her friends and family this week. That thought made her feel sad at the opportunities that were lost. "It's too bad we never got to all talk about it together."

Todd shrugged. "Tracy said the same thing when she and Doug were over this afternoon. They wanted to go with me to pick up your gift at the jeweler's, and then they came over to help me wrap it. I told her there's always the next time we're all together."

Christy realized that was why Doug and Tracy were at Todd's house when she called. They weren't having a special get-together and leaving her out. They were helping Todd with her present. Now she felt even worse about the things she had said to him on the phone. But that was in the past. Todd had already told her it was okay. She knew they needed to move forward and start fresh in this brand-new year.

"Thanks, Todd," Christy said, reaching over and squeezing his shoulder.

"Sure. You're welcome."

"I mean, thanks for the bracelet, but thanks, too, for not giving up on me, even though I acted like a brat."

"Hey, I already forgave you. Let's leave it back there, all right?" He nodded over his shoulder. "Let's give us a second chance."

They pulled up in front of Bob and Marti's, and Todd came around to open her door. Slipping his arm around her shoulders, they walked slowly to the front door.

Todd tilted his head back, looked up, and stopped walking. Christy put her arm around his waist and looked up, too. The night sky stretched above them like a long, extravagant garment of black velvet, dotted with thousands of glittering diamonds.

"It's beautiful," Christy murmured.

"You know," Todd said, "that's where God scatters our sins when we confess them to Him. He says, 'As far as the east is from the west,' that's how far He's removed from us all the stuff we've done wrong."

They gazed at the vastness in quiet awe.

"When I was little," Christy said softly, "I used to think that the sky at night was a big black blanket that separated heaven from earth, and the stars were a whole bunch of little pinholes that the angels poked in the blanket so they could look down on us."

Todd squeezed her shoulder and gave a little chuckle. "Sometimes, Christy, you totally amaze me."

"Oh yeah?" she said, pulling away just enough so she could face him. "Most of the time, Todd, you 'totally amaze me'!"

"Good," he replied, confidently pulling her back to his side and walking up to the front door. "That's the way it should be. Hey, do you think your aunt and uncle would mind if I went in, even though it's late? I left my mandolin in the living room."

"I'm sure it's okay," Christy said. "My aunt might even give you a sobriety test."

They both laughed and went in, finding her whole family still up, sitting in the den. As soon as they walked in, Dad looked at his watch.

"You're early," he said.

"Should we leave and come back?" Christy teased.

"Of course not!" Mom said, turning her head from her stretched-out position on the couch. "How was the party?"

"It was great!" Christy said. "We played some games, then roasted marshmallows outside over a fire pit. Doug brought a big box of sparklers, and that was really fun."

"I must say, that's a much better way to welcome the new year than to drink yourselves silly!" Marti commented. "You should be thankful for such good friends, Christy."

"I am," she said, smiling at Todd. "Believe me, I am."

Todd returned the smile and said, "I need to pick up my mandolin. Is it still in the living room?"

"Why, yes, it is," Marti said.

Then Todd did something that made Christy feel proud. He walked over and shook hands with her dad and with Bob, then kissed Marti on the cheek and thanked her for the dinner. He slapped high five to David and leaned over and gave Christy's mother a quick peck on the cheek, too.

"Thanks for letting me be a part of your family tonight," Todd said.

Perhaps only Christy knew how much being with family on the holidays meant to Todd.

"You're welcome at our house anytime," Marti said graciously. "And I mean that."

"Same goes for us," Dad said.

Christy couldn't believe her ears! *Is my father actually inviting Todd to come down to our house?*

"You'll have to come to Escondido sometime and see us," Dad said. Christy knew he meant it.

"Thanks. I'll do that. I'd better get going. Happy New Year, everyone." Todd slipped into the living room while Christy waited for him at the front door. With his mandolin in one hand,

Todd gave her a one-armed hug and said, "I guess I'll have to come down to Escondido sometime."

"You heard what my dad said. You're welcome anytime."

Todd opened the front door, then turned and said, "Well, I'll see you, then."

"Later?" Christy teased.

Todd smiled and said, "Yeah, later, Chris." He leaned over and gave her one of his warm, brotherly kisses on her temple, partly in her hair. Then, as he closed the door, he said with a slight wink, "Green apples, huh?"

The door was all the way closed before Christy understood, and when she did, she laughed aloud. Her heart felt as it never had before: warmed, happy, content.

"Don't worry, everybody! He only kissed her on the head," David reported in a blaring voice to the others in the den. His scrunched-up nose stuck out from around the corner.

"Why, you little hamster!" Christy yelled and chased him through the dining room and into the kitchen. "I'm going to short-circuit your bow tie!"

"Just try, Beetle Face," David challenged from behind the kitchen counter.

"That's enough, you two!" Dad's voice boomed from the hallway. "It's time for bed for both of you."

Regaining her dignity, Christy smoothed back her hair and paraded past her dad with David hot on her trail, still trying to torment her.

"Good night, everyone!" she called from the bottom stair. "And good night, David," she said, turning to face him. "I hope you don't dream about big black beetles that like to eat little hamsters!"

His face puckered up, and he said, "Oh yeah? Well, I hope

that . . ." He searched for some jab. "I hope that . . . that you don't dream at all!"

Christy turned and floated up the stairs, murmuring, "Who needs to dream?" *Tonight was real life, and it was better than any dream.*

Then, just to make sure tonight really happened, she reached for her wrist and ran her finger over the etched "Forever" on her smooth, gold bracelet. *Forever, Lord.* Her heart melted into the words as she prayed them. *No matter what happens, no matter what You've got planned for me, no matter how things end up for Todd and me, I want You to know that I am Yours. I'm Yours, God. Yours forever.*

Don't Miss These Captivating Stories in
THE CHRISTY MILLER SERIES

THE SIERRA JENSEN SERIES

If you've enjoyed reading about Christy Miller,
you'll love reading about Christy's friend Sierra Jensen.

#1 • Only You, Sierra
When her family moves to another state, Sierra dreads going to a new high school—until she meets Paul.

#2 • In Your Dreams
Just when events in Sierra's life start to look up—she even gets asked out on a date—Sierra runs into Paul.

#3 • Don't You Wish
Sierra is excited about visiting Christy Miller in California during Easter break. Unfortunately, her sister, Tawni, decides to go with her.

#4 • Close Your Eyes
Sierra experiences a sticky situation when Paul comes over for dinner and Randy shows up at the same time.

#5 • Without A Doubt
When handsome Drake reveals his interest in Sierra, life gets complicated.

#6 • With This Ring
Sierra couldn't be happier when she goes to Southern California to join Christy Miller and their friends for Doug and Tracy's wedding.

#7 • Open Your Heart
When Sierra's friend Christy Miller receives a scholarship from a university in Switzerland, she invites Sierra to go with her and Aunt Marti to visit the school.

#8 • Time Will Tell
After an exciting summer in Southern California and Switzerland, Sierra returns home to several unsettled relationships.

#9 • Now Picture This
When Sierra and Paul start corresponding, she imagines him as her boyfriend and soon begins neglecting her family and friends.

#10 • Hold On Tight
Sierra joins her brother and several friends on a road trip to Southern California to visit potential colleges.

#11 • Closer Than Ever
When Paul doesn't show up for her graduation party and news comes that a flight from London has crashed, Sierra frantically worries about the future.

#12 • Take My Hand
A costly misunderstanding leaves Sierra anxious as she says goodbye to Portland and heads off to California for her freshman year of college.